Twelve Stories for Summer

Twelve Stories for Summer

Linda Mansfield

A Restart Communications, LLC publication

First published in the United States by Linda Mansfield.

TWELVE STORIES FOR SUMMER

Copyright © 2017 by Linda Mansfield

This is a work of fiction. Names, characters, businesses, places, events and incidents are either the products of the author's imagination or used in a fictitious manner. Any resemblance to actual persons, living or dead, or actual events is purely coincidental.

ISBN: 978-0-9968617-0-0 (EPUB)

ISBN: 978-0-9968617-1-7 (MOBI)

ISBN: 978-0-9962433-9-1 (paperback)

ISBN: 978-0-9962433-8-4 (hardcover)

Cover art © Anyaberkut/Dollar Photo Club.

10 9 8 7 6 5 4 3 2 1

Dedication

*To Susan Shiffer; Barbara and Bob Ragonese; Andy Lally;
Brendan Cunnane; Tom and Pam Volk; John Heydenreich;
Marti Humphrey; Nena Ray; Anita Millican; Dave and
Laura Reininger; Tim and Sue Sopko; Amy Hall; Don and
Carole Bruce; Betsy Klasnick; Virginia Bruce; Joe and Lisa
Bruce; Maureen Handy; Dick, Connie and Geoff Dodge;
Tina LoSardo-Christie; Karen Mansfield; Janet McGehee;
Gary Mondschein; Lee Anne Patterson; Gene and Bonnie
Bare; Jack and Kathi Borsos; Jill Shamon and John Cole;
Jeret Schroeder; Debbie Deioma Danto; Wanda Devin;
Nick and Debbie Fornoro Jr.; Mike King; Mark Wingler;
Sam Schmidt; Kenny Brown and Cari Southworth; Scott
and Jill Logsdon; Ray and Brenda Quinn; Lee Bob and
Deanna Sedam; Barbara Burns, and the late Lani Nelson,
Joan and Sam Norris, and Bob Strauss.*

*These people helped me through a difficult time, and I'm
forever grateful.*

Contents

Reviews

Introduction

Indianapolis, Ind.

Summer is the traditional time for vacations, but many people are more busy than usual in the summertime. After trying to pack as much fun as possible into a short time span, often people need a vacation *after* their vacation.

"Twelve Stories for Summer" aims to give you a break. It's the third of four books in the "Two Good Feet" series. The series starts with "Stories for the 12 Days of Christmas," and proceeds with "Twelve Stories for Spring" and "Twelve Stories for Summer." It concludes with "Twelve Stories for Fall."

The goal of all four books is to provide stress relief and enjoyment for teenagers through senior citizens who enjoy quick reads. Each book contains a baker's dozen of fictional short stories that take far less time to read than a novel. Each story in each book is complete and can be read separately. However, if you choose to read all four books you'll get a glimpse into a complete year in the lives of many of the characters.

I hope you enjoy "Twelve Stories for Summer" whether you're reading it stretched out poolside or to kill time while you're waiting for someone or something. No matter where you squeeze these little stories into your life, I hope they provide a few moments of relaxation and enjoyment.

Linda Mansfield

LindaMansfieldBooks.com
Linda Mansfield — Author on Facebook
@RestartLMAuthor on Twitter

Please join our mailing list via the form
on LindaMansfieldBooks.com's home page
and receive a *free* short story!

Authors depend on good reviews.
If you enjoy this book, please consider posting
a short review at the outlet where you purchased it.
Thank you!

1

Girl Meets Boy, Maybe Sort of

Kathy Simpson wiped perspiration from her forehead, reset her sunglasses on her nose, and took a sip of lukewarm coffee from a white foam cup she had been cradling between her legs as she drove. Fulfilling her car-pooling obligations to deliver her son Luke and three of his friends to swimming class at a nearby state park gave her a chance to eavesdrop on their conversations. As a single mom, Kathy needed every advantage available.

Luke's friends seemed as wholesome as he was, and Kathy wanted to keep it that way. Alcohol and drugs didn't seem to be attractive to them yet, and they were indifferent to girls. At the moment they were debating the skill sets of the current pitchers for the Chicago Cubs.

Kathy wasn't sure which was louder — the four soon-to-be fifth-grade boys crammed into her green compact car, or its muffler, which had been acting up since last winter. The car's air conditioning hadn't worked when she bought the car used, so all the windows were cranked down as far as they'd go. Any air available during a humid afternoon in late July in rural Indiana would be welcome.

Kathy knew she looked a sight. The foundation and lip gloss she'd applied before breakfast had slid off her face hours ago. Her shoulder-length brown hair was in the standard ponytail she used when serving tables at a local restaurant. A blue cap advertising the restaurant, The Brown Jug, was jammed on her head. The ponytail was poking out of the hole above the cap's blue plastic strap at the back used to adjust its width. She'd chucked her apron, and there were splotches of ketchup and some unknown brown stain on the lime green T-shirt she wore over faded jeans. The T-shirt advertised Ben's Honey-Making Supplies. It featured a giant bee hovering over a beehive, and proclaimed "We'll Give You a Honey of a Deal!" in script lettering. The T-shirt was too big for her lean frame so she'd knotted the end of it, creating a big bump over her right hip.

In contrast, her only child could have been modeling for some magazine cover, although he'd taken no time to create his good appearance. Blessed with his absent father's long blond hair and sapphire-blue eyes, he was wearing red swim trunks and a navy-blue polo shirt. Kathy knew she was biased, but she wasn't the only one in town who thought Luke Simpson could be a model or an actor someday.

Luke's aspirations tended more towards becoming a professional athlete. He loved all sports, and he was pining for a dirt bike and a go-kart. That was impossible on Kathy's income, but she could handle swimming lessons.

She had car-pool duty each Tuesday at 2 p.m. to deliver Luke and three of his friends to swim practice at the lake at Hemlock State Park a few miles outside of town. Luckily her boss at The Brown Jug allowed her the time off during her shift on Tuesdays, and she didn't start her job as a cashier at the town's dollar store until 7 p.m. Her mom usually did the other half of her run, picking up the kids and delivering them to their respective homes after the two-hour lesson concluded.

Kathy appreciated her mother's help. It was tough paying all the bills even with two jobs. There were rumblings that the manager of the dollar store might be resigning soon, and if that happened she should be in line for that position with her seniority.

She'd been juggling so many things for so long she couldn't remember the last time she did anything for herself. About the only thing she did for her own entertainment was read romance paperbacks in bed before she turned off the light. It was an escape, but to Kathy they were fairy tales that made her own prospects for love seem even more unattainable. Mainsville was a small town with few single men her age. She didn't have time for a social life anyway.

Kathy sighed and tried to count her blessings. The swimming lessons were part of the state park's outreach efforts. She didn't know who would teach Luke to swim without them. Something about submerging her head under water terrified her, although she did know how to float. Ron Martin, the park's only ranger and the lake's only lifeguard, offered the lessons for a nominal charge thanks to a stipend from the state.

About a mile from the park entrance a doe leaped out of a cornfield next to the road, forcing Kathy to slam on the brakes. Her coffee cup went flying, dousing most of its contents on her T-shirt. She pulled over to the shoulder of the road to sop up what she could. The boys were fine, and thought the whole thing was hilarious. She gave them a look, but they were having too much fun to notice.

As Kathy pulled into the lake's parking lot, she didn't recognize the big, blue SUV already parked there. Its air conditioner must have worked because the car's windows were up. She could see, if not hear, its driver and his three young passengers. They were girls about the same age as her carload of boys, and they were singing at the top of their lungs. The driver, a man about her age, was playing an invisible drum set. Kathy couldn't help but smile. He grinned sheepishly and waved.

After the boys yelled goodbye and tumbled out of her car, she pulled out of her space in the parking lot. With her schedule, there was no time to dally.

She'd become accustomed to the noise her faulty muffler made, but suddenly it and most of her tailpipe dropped to the ground in a rusty heap with a loud thud. Some of the tailpipe was still attached to the front third of her car's undercarriage.

Kathy put the car into park with a groan, lowered her head, and turned the engine off. Clearly she wasn't going anywhere for a while. The park was silent now her car was quiet. Kathy imagined the local fauna was standing in the bushes surrounding the parking lot like concerned passerby, wondering what was going to happen next.

Luke trotted back to see what the problem was.

"It's OK; I'll call AAA; you go on ahead with your swimming lesson," Kathy told him.

Luke could sense she was upset, and being more mature than his years, he stuck around.

Kathy was in the car and on her cell phone with the dispatcher, who was somewhere in Kansas, when the driver of the blue SUV approached them. He was taller than she'd thought. He had thick, black hair, with some gray at his temples. He wore casual, tan pants, and a blue-plaid, cotton sports shirt. He smiled a welcome to her as he and Luke chatted near the front of her car.

Engrossed in her call, Kathy didn't notice the rich perfume of the pines surrounding the parking lot, and she only heard the end of their conversation.

"Mom is strange," she heard her son confide softly to the man.

I thought we were in this together, Luke! Kathy thought, shocked.

"Don't say that!" the man admonished. "Everyone is a little quirky. Don't say your mother is strange."

"No; she's strange from my dad," Luke explained in a loud whisper.

"Oh! Estranged!" the man realized after a beat, giving Luke a weak smile. "That's good to know," he murmured.

Kathy pretended she hadn't overheard. She knew Luke didn't like to think of her as a divorcee. Luke still hoped his father would come back, but neither of them knew where he was.

"Big Al from Al's Towing will be here in about a half-hour," she announced. "I had to go through the AAA system and not call his cell so there would be no charge. I knew he was working today, because I waited on him this morning at breakfast," she added. "He always has the working man's special, with three eggs, sunny side up." She had no idea why she was talking so much.

"Ah, the joys of small-town living, where everyone knows everyone's business," said the man as he moved to the driver's side window and thrust his right hand through it. "I'm Dave Shepherd," he said. "I just moved here with my daughter, Jill, to take a job at the power plant."

"It's nice to meet you, Dave. Welcome to Mainsville," Kathy said while shaking his hand. "I'm Kathy Simpson, and that's my son, Luke."

"It's nice to meet you both," Dave responded. "My daughter, Jill, is the one with the purple swimsuit," he said, pointing her out.

"You go along, Luke; I'll wait for Al; there's no need for you to miss your lesson," Kathy told her son.

"OK!" Luke said as he bounced off, leaving Kathy and Dave alone.

"Really, Al will be here soon; you don't have to wait," Kathy told Dave, but he would hear none of it. Before long Kathy learned he was also divorced, he had sole custody of his daughter, and he'd moved into the old Cunningham house about a month ago. Kathy knew where the Cunningham's brick ranch was. The couple had gone to her church, and had finally moved to Florida last fall for good after years of being snowbirds.

After a few minutes of conversation, Dave learned Kathy held two jobs to make ends meet, and her funds were tight. Despite her disheveled appearance, he could tell she was attractive. Something about her situation and the determined set of her shoulders made him want to help her. He found himself making her an offer she couldn't refuse.

"If you buy the parts, I'll install your new muffler and tailpipe," he told her.

"Oh, I couldn't let you do that."

Dave looked at her with his head cocked at an angle. "Well, in exchange I'd like a guided tour of Mainsville's hot spots when I'm done."

"Mainsville doesn't have any hot spots. You can see everything there is to see in less than 10 minutes."

Dave could see this was going to be harder than he thought. "It's just that I don't know many people here yet."

Kathy looked at him, surprised. "You mean like in a date?" she blurted out, fear in her eyes.

"Well, maybe sort of," Dave said. "Think of it as two single parents getting together to compare notes."

Kathy's life was wrapped up in being the best single mom possible. It had been a long time since she'd been on a date, even if this would only be sort of one.

She looked at Dave, and she looked at the coffee stain on her T-shirt. She found herself answering without her typical mental torture of weighing all the reasons why she should or shouldn't do something.

"I'll be glad to show you around," she heard someone say in her voice.

Dave spoke quickly before she had a chance to change her mind. "Do you want to have your car towed to my house? Most of my garage is set up, and I have ramps there."

"Well...." Kathy said slowly. "I live over The Brown Jug restaurant. Could you bring the ramps over and do the work in the alley? There's plenty of room, and..." her voice trailed off. "It's just that this is a small town, and if my car is at your house overnight, people will talk."

"Ah! I should have thought of that," Dave said sympathetically. "Of course! I'll bring everything over in my SUV. I'll help you order the parts; should I call you as soon as I get back from taking the girls home?"

It was settled. Phone numbers were exchanged, and Al arrived about five minutes later. After parking the tow truck in front of Kathy's car, he lowered himself out of the cab with a thud. He wore greasy denim coveralls over a gray T-shirt. Yellow suspenders designed like a carpenter's measuring tape bulged over his large belly.

"Hey, girl! Everyone in town has been waiting for that muffler to finally fall off so you'd get a new one and we'd all have some peace and quiet again!" he teased her.

"Everything in its own time," Kathy shot back, unruffled.

Al started the process of loading her car on his truck while Kathy and Dave looked on. After Al attached the final chain and the car slid onto the flatbed, Kathy said a polite goodbye to Dave and climbed into the passenger side of the big red tow truck. They might pass her mom on her way to the park to pick up the kids, but at least she had a plan.

She also sort of had a date.

And as she and Al drove away and left Dave to his own devices, for the first time in a long time Kathy felt her luck might finally be changing for the better.

2

A Long Island
Fourth of July

Roger Markowitz rubbed a mosquito bite on his left arm and then motioned for his companion, 10-year-old Harry Montgomery, to go ahead of him as the light changed and they stepped off the curb. Their destination this hot morning was the annual Fourth of July Parade in Southampton, New York. Harry smiled with anticipation and did as he was told. And behind Roger, with the stealth of all predatory animals, an unassuming middle-aged man wearing a baseball cap and sunglasses reached into Roger's back pocket and stole his wallet as they crossed the street, without anyone noticing him at all.

Roger was earning brownie points by looking after Harry today. Harry's father, who was his boss at a major accounting firm in Manhattan, had been called away to a meeting with an important client in Switzerland. Harry's mother was in the middle of a two-week stay at a spa in Scottsdale, Arizona. Harry's nanny had been in Paris all week to attend her younger sister's wedding that very day. The family's housekeeper wasn't up to outings. Since Roger had been renting a small cottage this summer in East Hampton anyway, he volunteered to spend the day with his boss's son, who was set on attending Southampton's popular holiday parade.

Roger had met Harry a couple of times in the past, when the nanny brought him into the city and they stopped by the office. Roger was struck by the boy's maturity. Roger had no particular interest in children, but he'd decided it wouldn't hurt to interact with them now and then after a chance encounter with an intriguing little girl on a flight to Cancun last December.

So late yesterday afternoon Roger had inched his rented Porsche through the traffic headed to Long Island, suffering through it like everyone else. When he finally reached his cottage, he baited his eight wire crab traps with chicken legs he'd purchased at a grocery store in town, and placed the traps in the water nearby. He ordered a pizza for dinner, slept a few hours, and picked up Harry at the Montgomery estate at 8 a.m. the next morning. The estate was located in East Hampton's summer colony, where the homes sold for upwards of $20 million.

Harry was sitting on the marble stairs in the foyer, waiting for him. After exchanging pleasantries with the housekeeper, they were off.

The Porsche impressed Harry. After fielding a few of his questions during the half-hour ride to Southampton, Roger realized Harry knew more about the car than he did.

They were lucky to find a parking spot on a side street. After locking the car, they headed towards the parade route. Along the way, Harry talked Roger into stopping at a small coffee shop for an iced coffee.

The pair looked like close relatives as they sat on black metal chairs, sipping their coffees. Roger, who was tall and had medium-brown hair, was wearing khaki pants, a mint green polo shirt, and brown sandals, all purchased from Bloomingdale's. Harry was wearing tan cargo shorts, a bright green Lacoste polo that caught the flecks of green in his brown eyes, and dark brown, custom-made sandals that matched his hair.

After the coffee break and the short walk to the parade route during which Roger became an unsuspecting robbery victim, they settled along the curb to watch the parade. Harry sat on the curb itself, while Roger stood behind him until a lady offered him one of her lawn chairs. It was supposed to be for her teenage granddaughter, but she called her on her cell phone to say she wasn't going to make it to the parade like she'd thought.

Roger had to hand it to the parade organizers. For a small town, they went all out to celebrate America's birthday. A man wearing a sports shirt featuring a large American flag gave them and other onlookers small American flags to wave. There were local floats, bands, and lots of antique cars and antique fire trucks. At one point one unit fired off an old mobile cannon right on the street.

A band of bagpipers was marching by when Roger felt into the right pocket of his pants and discovered his wallet was missing. He didn't say a word, but panic gripped his eyes.

He checked his other pocket. His keys and cell phone were there, but his wallet wasn't.

He knew he hadn't left it at his cottage; he'd paid the bill at the coffee shop with cash. He didn't think it dropped out of his pocket on its own. His pants had deep pockets. But lost or stolen, the bottom line was he had no idea where his cash, three favorite credit cards, his driver's license, and a few other important cards were.

Roger's feelings were in a tizzy. First there was the disconcerting thought of being away from home without any money or credit cards. Blame came next. If he'd lost the wallet on his own his boss was sure to find out about it from Harry, and it didn't portray much responsibility. If he'd been the victim of a robbery, he felt violated and mad.

All those thoughts were screaming for attention, and Roger didn't know which one to address first.

Don't panic he admonished himself.

Roger quietly thumbed through his cell phone's directory and pressed the number for a service he'd purchased annually for years but had never used. His credit card numbers were on file there, and they'd alert the credit card companies immediately to put stops on all his cards and issue him new ones. They'd even notify the New York Department of Motor Vehicles for him, and apply for a replacement driver's license.

The call took less than 5 minutes, but Harry heard the whole thing.

"Somebody stole your wallet?" he asked when Roger hung up.

"I think so," Roger admitted. "But we're not going to let that spoil our day."

"OK," Harry said, with the assurance of a child who believes what he's told. "My mom and dad would be freaking out if that happened to them, though."

"I try to avoid freaking out." Roger shook his head. "I don't have any cash now though."

"Don't worry; I have $300 from my allowance on me, and a Gold American Express card."

"You get $300 a month in allowance?" Roger said, dumbstruck. He hadn't considered the fact Harry would have a credit card either.

"No, $350," Harry said without missing a beat.

A Dixieland band in front of them made any further conversation impossible for the next four minutes.

While they played, Roger did a search on his phone and found the number for the local police department. After some politicians in convertibles had replaced the band, he made one more call and reported the lost wallet to the local authorities. If it was stolen, he wanted the police to know about it. If it was lost, there was always the chance someone honest would find it and turn it in.

About 45 minutes later, after an Elvis impersonator with a wireless microphone sang "God Bless America" with an elderly veteran in the crowd, the end of the parade sauntered by them.

"What's next on our schedule?" Roger asked Harry.

"We could drive the Porsche to the Smith Haven Mall and check out the Apple watches at the Apple store," he suggested.

"Hum." Roger made some quick calculations. "That would take us a little over an hour each way, but if that's what you want to do, we'll do it. Let's get lunch here first though, to save time."

They partook of a handy food truck for a quick lunch, and of course considering the situation, Harry paid. Roger had a barbecue sandwich and lemonade. Harry chose two corn dogs and lemonade as well. He considered a funnel cake but discarded that idea when he thought about the mess powdered sugar would make on his shirt. He made a production out of ordering the lemonade, returning the first one and insisting the second one have far less pulp.

During the drive to Lake Grove, Roger learned Harry was a computer geek, and he seemed to have a clear vision of his career path despite his young age. He hadn't made his final decision on the college he'd attend yet and he didn't read many books, but he never missed an issue of "Forbes" or "Entrepreneur" magazines. After college, he planned to start his own technology company and then sell it for millions if not billions of dollars.

Roger learned Harry was popular with girls his age too, as during the course of the trip he received three text messages from girls he knew.

"They prank call me a lot," Harry said with the nonchalance an actor might use to describe fans' requests for autographs and selfies.

The shopping trip was uneventful for Roger, who was just doing it to please Harry. It was obvious Harry had done this trip many times in the past, as the young people manning the Genius Bar greeted him by his first name. In a few minutes he was engrossed with the Apple watch offerings, learning more from one of the salespeople and asking questions about apps, battery life, and the different styles and options available.

Roger found a stool and waited for him patiently. Harry was shopping, not buying, and soon he told Roger he was ready to go. "They don't have the watch I want yet, and I'm still deciding on a few things," Harry told him.

"What's next?" Roger asked.

"Oh, I don't know; I guess let's go home."

They made a quick stop at Hollister, which was next to the Apple store, and headed to East Hampton.

"I was going to take you out to eat tonight, but since I don't have my wallet, how about we see if we can rustle up some crabs?" Roger suggested on the way back.

"Cool," was Harry's response, so Roger took him back to his cottage. After quick trips to the bathroom, they grabbed some chicken legs in a plastic bag from the refrigerator and a bushel basket outside the cottage's back door, and headed to the spot near the neighborhood pier where Roger had left his crab traps.

They rolled up their pants legs, waded out a few feet, found the traps, and pulled them up. The chicken pieces had done the trick, as all but one trap had at least one crab in it. They had 19 crabs in all.

"Cool!" Harry repeated after they waded back on shore and dumped the crabs into the basket. "We got a lot of them!"

That's when Roger noticed a white man fishing on the pier.

"Are you having any luck?" Roger asked him casually.

"Not yet," the man said.

"Well, you're welcome to some of these," Roger responded. "Harry and I can eat about a dozen, and you can have the rest."

"Well, thank you; I don't mind if I do," the man said, and after taking seven crabs from them and putting them in his metal bucket, he was off.

Although Harry had been summering on Long Island all his life, this was his first encounter with crabbing. Roger showed him how to rebait the traps, and they put them back into the water before heading back to the cottage with their catch.

The cottage was set up for crabbers, as the back yard had a gas burner and a picnic table designed for the job. The building was done in saltbox style. It was suitable only for summer living, as it had no source of heat.

After rinsing off their feet with the garden hose next to the table, Roger put some water in the bottom of a big aluminum pot already on the burner to steam the crabs. He didn't use any seasoning but he brought plenty of melted butter from the kitchen, where he'd microwaved it in two small bowls perfect for dipping. When the crabs were steamed he removed them with tongs and dumped them on the picnic table, which he'd covered with newspaper. He showed Harry how to crack the crabs open, and the feast began.

A comfortable silence came over the pair as they worked to uncover the meat and ate. Later, after they'd cleaned the table and the dishes, they talked about some financial news, Harry's plans for the rest of the summer, and Harry's dad's polo team. Harry played a game on his phone while Roger did a crossword puzzle he'd found on a sheet of newspaper that hadn't yet become a tablecloth, and another comfortable silence came upon them as the sun sank in the west and the water before them became darker. A few bugs circled an outside light near the cottage that came on automatically, while others made popping noises as they hit a bug zapper swinging from an old pine tree a few paces away.

Roger drove Harry home in time for Harry to watch the Macy's fireworks display on TV. Harry had nodded off a little in the car, but he thanked Roger sincerely when he turned to him after the house-keeper opened the front door.

"Thank you, Roger; I had a lot of fun!" Harry said. "It was the best weekend ever! I never get to do what I want to do on the weekends. This was really neat!"

"Maybe we will do it again sometime," Roger answered, pleased.

"You're a kind man, Mr. Markowitz," the housekeeper said, nodding her thanks. "Just spending time with a child is important."

The following morning Roger pulled up his crab traps before the long trip back to the city. He only caught five crabs in them this time, and two of them were females, so he let them go rather than postpone his trip back to the city any further. As he did, he noticed a plastic bag taped watertight with duct tape at the bottom of one of the traps. It was wrapped so tight he had to open it with his crab knife.

He was stunned to find his wallet inside.

He pulled it open and looked at the contents. He wasn't sure how much money he'd had in it when he left for the parade yesterday, but it looked like he was only about $20 short. A man who regretted his actions and was trying to make amends had returned the rest of the money, his credit cards, his driver's license, and his other important cards.

That's a new twist on Robin Hood Roger thought as he began the long trip back to Manhattan about an hour later. *Steal from the rich and give back what you don't spend right away.*

But Harry was right; it was a great holiday.

3

What Goes Up Eventually Comes Down

Josh Martin squirmed a little on the double seat of the school bus, trying to find a spot where the backs of his sunburned legs wouldn't stick to its dark green vinyl covering. He balanced himself on the seat ahead of him with his right hand, but looked down quickly when he saw Frankie Jones ambling up the aisle, straight for him.

Josh knew Frankie wouldn't sit with him. He knew Frankie would find a seat near him, however, and the bullying would start.

"Hey, it's Baby Josh! How ya doing?" Frankie asked him, as if on cue. "Are you going to cry today?" he added, drawing the word 'cry' out for emphasis as he slipped into the seat behind Josh. Joe Walker, who had been sitting there, moved towards the window to make room without a word.

Frankie and Josh had never been friends, but Frankie's bullying got worse after an unfortunate incident at last year's Christmas Eve church service had left Josh in tears. Josh wanted desperately to put the incident behind him. Frankie was determined to remind Josh about it as often as possible.

More kids poured onto the bus. Josh was relieved when Marti Cook, one of the chaperones, sat beside him. Josh didn't like the term 'babysitter,' but Marti often stayed with him when his parents went out. Everybody in town liked Marti. She had agreed to teach the second-graders at this year's Bible School for the Chapel Hill Baptist Church. Today's bus trip to Summerworld Amusement Park was the culmination of the two-week curriculum this year, and it had been highly anticipated by the kids since they learned of it. Josh had been a little worried about Frankie during the trip all along, but he wouldn't dare do anything with Marti within earshot.

The bus lurched forward and made its way out of the church parking lot, down a few streets of the small town, and onto the expressway. The trip would take about 45 minutes because Chapel Hill was in the middle of nowhere.

Marti scrolled through her phone, and Josh watched the fields of corn and soybeans flash by the window as the bus lumbered down the highway like a giant caterpillar making its way across a branch.

Marti reached into her backpack and pulled out a book, "Twelve Stories for Summer," which was the third book in a four-book series. She'd already read the first two, she was enjoying this one, and she was eager to read the fourth book, "Twelve Stories for Fall," when that season rolled around.

"Are you looking forward to Summerworld?" Marti asked him when she looked up from her book.

Josh nodded and gave her a shy smile.

"What are you going to ride first?"

"Maybe the Firecracker."

"Oh! Not me! I'd get sick on that!"

Josh smiled. He was OK on rides that moved fast, but he didn't like heights.

The church bus finally lumbered into the amusement park's parking lot. Pastor Simmons rose from his seat in the front, thanked the teachers and kids for another great Bible School, and told them all to have fun. Marti and the other chaperones distributed the ride tickets, the time to be back on board the bus was emphasized, the buddy system was encouraged, and the kids were set loose.

Josh took the three steps off the bus gingerly due to his sunburn. Most of the kids darted off towards the rides immediately, but Joe Walker had stayed behind too.

"Frankie Jones is a jerk," Joe confided. "Do you want to do the rides with me?"

"Yes! Thanks!" Josh said, relieved.

Joe and his family had moved from Colorado to Chapel Hill this spring. Josh had seen him in school, but Joe was in the grade behind him and lived across town so they hadn't had many chances to interact. As far as Josh knew, Joe hadn't heard about the fuss on Christmas Eve.

"What do you want to do first?" Joe asked.

"The Firecracker!" Josh replied, and they were off. Once they'd ridden the Firecracker, they moved from one ride to another as fast as they could tear off their ride tickets and the lines would permit.

A little before the time they were all to meet in one of the picnic pavilions for lunch, Joe suggested they ride the Ferris wheel.

"I'm not too good with heights," Josh admitted.

"It'll be OK; you'll love it!" Joe said encouragingly.

"I'm not so sure."

"You won't know until you try!" Joe pointed out.

"Well…," Josh relented. Before he could think about it anymore the two boys were in line and then stepping into a mint green car.

Josh's sunburn made him uncomfortable, but he tried to be brave as a scary-looking man with tattoos and a long beard pushed a metal bar in place at the front of their car to secure them inside. The man was wearing a tank shirt. He'd slipped a pack of cigarettes under one of the straps, making him look like he had some sort of large tumor. The car swung in place a few times, and Josh hoped for the best.

In the beginning it wasn't too bad, because there were lots of stops as kids got in the remaining cars. Josh tried not to look over the countryside as they rose higher, but he could feel his stomach churn.

"You look a little green!" Joe pointed out.

"Yeah, I don't feel so good. I hope this is over soon."

Unfortunately, the ride was just getting started. It wasn't full, but the operator was in a good mood and he liked to give his patrons their money's worth.

"Oh…." Josh said, his head dropping to his chest as he tried hard not to vomit as the car rose higher and went faster. It made at least five revolutions at speed, with Josh getting greener each time.

Suddenly the ride came to a stop with the boys' car at the top.

"Oh… Don't swing the car," Josh admonished Joe.

"I won't. Don't spit up on me," Joe ordered.

"I'll try not to."

"This is cool!" Joe said as he looked over the countryside. "I can see a bunch of cows!"

"Good," said Josh, who was staring at the bottom hem of his T-shirt in an effort not to hurl.

"You really don't like being up high, do you?"

"No," Josh said weakly.

Seconds turned into minutes as the boys waited for the ride to resume.

"What's taking them so long? We've been here on top for a while," Joe pointed out.

A few more minutes passed. Josh was making a point to look at his sneakers and not the view. He counted eight holes on the sneakers where the laces went through. Then, like an investigator researching the scene of a crime, he counted and noted the 32 small holes in the fabric on either side for air to pass through.

"We should have been moving by now," Joe observed.

More minutes passed.

"What's going on?" Josh asked his friend, looking up from his feet for an instant.

"There's a golf cart down there now, and a bunch of people standing around and looking up at us," Joe reported. "I think we might be stuck."

"Oh no," Josh said weakly.

And stuck they were. The minutes turned into an hour, and that hour turned into two.

"I'm hungry, and I sort of have to go to the bathroom," Joe confided.

"Well you're out of luck," Josh pointed out. "Hopefully they'll get this thing fixed soon."

More time passed and that possibility grew more unlikely.

"I think we're really stuck," Joe said, restating the obvious. "Hey, there's a fire truck down there, and two TV trucks!"

"Do you think we're going to be on the news?" Josh asked.

"Maybe!"

"What if we miss the bus?" Josh wondered aloud, thinking fondly of a home he wasn't sure he'd ever see again.

"They'll wait for us," Joe reassured him.

"It's hot. I'm thirsty. And I wish I'd brought my baseball cap," Josh continued. "The sun sure is hot. That's probably because we're even closer to it than usual."

"Well, we're not that much closer," Joe replied, and even Josh grinned.

"I guess we need to make the best of it," Josh conceded. "If I can survive this, maybe I'll cure my fear of heights."

"That's the spirit, Josh!"

As more minutes passed, Josh's gaze cautiously rose once again from his sneakers to his new friend's face.

"I think I'm feeling a little better," Josh said tentatively.

"Great!" Joe said. "I think they're coming for us."

He was right. A bucket on the fire truck's crane had already reached the first stranded passengers, who were carefully climbing aboard it.

Josh and Joe watched the whole thing and waited their turn.

Another hour passed as the rescue progressed. In response to the humidity of the day, several bolts of lightning flashed in some angry gray clouds in the distance as the firemen continued their work.

Eventually everyone was back on Mother Earth except for Josh and Joe.

"We're next!" Joe told Josh.

"Yes, but I don't think they can reach us," Josh told him soberly. "The ladder won't reach that high."

Unfortunately, he was right.

"At least they know we're here," Joe reminded Josh. "They'll figure something out."

Another half hour passed. Several more bolts of lightning cracked the skyline, promising even more danger and jangling their nerves further.

"Maybe they almost have the ride fixed," Josh said, trying to be optimistic. "I hope so, because we missed lunch." He was surprised he was even thinking about food. His stomach, which had been queasy a little bit ago, seemed OK now.

"I really have to go to the bathroom," Joe confided.

"Try to hold it a little longer," Josh said. "They'll think of something. Let's talk about something else."

"Like what?" Joe wanted to know.

"I don't know," Josh said. "Maybe we could sing some of the songs we learned in Bible School."

"OK; let's try."

The boys launched into several songs and hummed the melody when they couldn't remember the words. Josh made up a whole new verse to one of them, which impressed Joe.

Far below them, the assembled crowd caught the strains of some of the songs.

"Good for them!" Marti told one of the reporters standing by for any updates. "They're singing songs we learned at Bible School!"

About 15 minutes later, everyone heard something else too. It was the sounds of a helicopter not too far away.

"Hey, Josh! The Army is coming for us!" Joe cried.

It was true. A helicopter from the nearest National Guard base was approaching from the north.

"How cool is that?" Joe said excitedly.

"Cool," Josh replied, but terror struck him as he wondered how the rescue would be carried out. He'd seen soldiers lowered from a helicopter by a tiny canvas ladder a few times on TV. "I don't think I can do the ladder thing," Josh told Joe.

"I don't think I can either," Joe agreed. "Maybe we can stay here until they fix the Ferris wheel."

"I don't think we're going to get a vote," Josh said wisely.

As both boys watched in awe, the helicopter stayed in place above them and a soldier was lowered towards them on a ladder, like they'd seen on TV.

"Hi, boys!" the soldier yelled above the noise of the helicopter when he got close.

"Hi!" they yelled in unison.

"I can't do the ladder thing, Josh!" Joe said.

"Yes you can; I'm the one who is afraid of heights, and I'm going to do it," Josh told him bravely. "If I can do it, you can too."

"Who wants to go first?" the soldier hollered, dangling beside them.

"Not me!" Joe said.

"OK; I'll go, and you can watch me," Josh said.

The soldier pulled two bottles of water out of his pockets and gave one to each boy.

"Who wants to go first?" the soldier repeated.

"I'll go," Josh replied.

The soldier buckled him into a harness and clipped the whole thing onto the ladder and also onto a similar harness he was wearing.

"Either look up or look at me; don't look down!" the soldier ordered.

Noticing Josh's eyes were already screwed shut, he added, "Not looking at all is a way to go too!" with a smile.

"There's nothing to it; up we go!" he said seconds later, and he held Josh tight as they both began to be pulled into the body of the helicopter.

Josh decided it was now or never to get over his fear of heights, and he opened his eyes. It seemed like an eternity, but in less than two minutes he was inside the helicopter, standing in a safe place, and other soldiers were unhooking his harness.

"Good job! I'll be back with your buddy in a minute!" the soldier who had rescued him told him.

In a few minutes the whole procedure was repeated, and Joe and Josh were reunited. The helicopter made a large circle and landed in a cornfield next to the parking lot. As the boys watched, the crowd that had been watching from the ground ran as fast as they could towards the field, and approached the helicopter once its blades stopped spinning.

Josh and Joe's first helicopter ride was followed shortly by their first appearance on the evening news.

"Here are the brave boys who were at the top of the Ferris wheel!" said Connie Henderson, the shapely blonde reporter from Channel 8. "Can you tell us about the experience?"

Joe looked at the microphone thrust in front of him, and gave credit where credit was due.

"Josh is afraid of heights, but he was very brave and helped me be strong enough to go with the soldier!" he said excitedly. "We're OK, but we want to go to the bathroom and eat all at the same time!"

Josh looked at his new friend appreciatively. "We helped each other, and we're glad the soldiers came to save us," he said.

"Yes! Thank you to the U.S. National Guard!" Joe agreed.

After a quick ride in a golf cart to the restrooms inside the amusement park's entrance followed by some chicken fingers at the only concession stand still open, Josh and Joe boarded the church bus and took a seat. They were late of course, but so was everyone else.

Frankie, intrigued by the helicopter, had been among the people in the crowd in the cornfield, and he'd heard the news interview live in person.

"Good job, kid!" he told Josh as he walked by, headed for a seat at the back of the bus.

Josh and Joe, who were at the end of Day 1 of a friendship that would continue the rest of their lives, smiled at each other and settled in for the ride home.

4

The Further Transformation Of Jeb Mitchell

Jeb Mitchell shifted his over-300-pound bulk from one side to the other, bit his lower lip, and tried not to breathe. Sweat poured from every pore of his 17-year-old body due to the humidity of summer in the South and his tight confines. He was stuffed into a tiny, window-less, and smelly bathroom in the basement of Sadie Tate's old farm-house in the backwoods of Kentucky. He was about to reach into a rusty pipe clogged with God-only-knew-what, and he didn't like it one bit.

Jeb rolled his eyes, stalling for time. He'd spent several weekends working to pay for this 'opportunity' he now faced as a volunteer on a church mission trip. To make matters worse, he'd had to come up with some extra money to help pay for this trip, which was taking a full week of his summer vacation between his junior and senior years of high school.

His previous plan of lying around the Mitchell family's house in the suburbs of Louisville all summer doing nothing seemed infinitely better than this.

He wasn't sure how he'd gotten this assignment. Maybe the fact his father was a plumber had something to do with it. Jeb rarely helped his dad on jobs, but perhaps he'd absorbed some knowledge from him. He was confident he was the best person in his group to do this job and it had to be done, so he reached in.

"Yuck!" he said, drawing out the word as his fingers clasped something soft, damp, and disgusting.

This wasn't just a clog. From the tiny feces and the gray fur woven among twigs, brown hair that was probably human, and a sliver of bar soap, he'd uncovered the remains of a mouse nest tangled in other debris.

He followed the first 'Yuck' with another one, wiped his hands on a rag that had been stuck in his back pocket, and reported back to the adult leader, Philip Barker, who was outside helping other kids saw two-by-fours for a new deck.

"The pipe is too brittle to repair; the whole line needs to be replaced," Jeb announced. "I saw some PVC pipe in the truck. I'll go get it."

"Thanks, Jeb," Phil said. "Let me know if you can't find it."

With so little room to work, Jeb continued on the plumbing detail single-handedly. He wasn't sure how he knew how to do it, but less than an hour later he was done.

"Jeb, we have peanut-butter sandwiches for lunch," said his neighbor, Caroline Brady, after she ventured down the basement stairs to check on him. Although she didn't know it, Caroline was the reason

Jeb had undergone a self-improvement campaign this year, and she was the reason he was on this trip. When he found out Caroline was going to spend a whole week of summer vacation on a church mission trip, Jeb had signed up just to spend more time with her.

At the time he didn't know it would include this stinky plumbing detail.

The group had arrived in Appalachia the night before, driving from Louisville in three rented buses. On the sides of each bus were plastic banners advertising 'Bethel Methodist Church.'

'Home' for the week would be a small rural high school with no air conditioning. The girls were sleeping on cots in the school's gym that were lined up like a field hospital. The boys were using sleeping bags in the hallways. Blankets, duffle bags and backpacks were thrown about, and clothes hung from the handles of lockers. It looked like a hurricane had swept through the school.

Boys' and girls' locker rooms flanked opposite sides of the gym, so showering, brushing teeth and similar drills were already segregated.

Breakfast, a grab-before-you-go deal, and dinner would be served in the school's cafeteria. Lunch would be sandwiches, soft drinks, and water brought to each work site.

At least Caroline was in his work group. She was working on the deck. She wasn't as grimy as he was, but her T-shirt was still stained with sweat.

A gray-haired, elderly woman named Sadie owned the property, and she'd welcomed the group to her cluttered home, which had the peculiar odor of poverty about it.

Sadie's unmarried and unemployed daughter, Penny, lived with her, as did Penny's three young children. When the church group arrived that morning, all five were watching "Judge Judy" on a huge, black TV that took up one entire end of their living room. Its large size, modern look, and state-of-the-art screen screamed in defiance of the home's rundown and cluttered nature. The volunteers had been warned to be polite and non-judgmental, and so far they were all complying.

Jeb washed up by using a green garden hose attached to an outdoor faucet near the porch. Caroline saw him and offered a clean towel.

"Thanks!" Jeb said, and added a quick "Be careful!" to Sadie, who was tottering towards them with a big, light-blue metal pan filled with scraps she'd generated while peeling potatoes.

"May I help you?" he asked Sadie, who accepted his assistance gratefully.

"They're for Lucy, our sow, who is in the pen beside the barn," Sadie said. "I'll show you where she is," she added, fumbling with something in the pocket of her faded apron, which was a light blue color with large, pink cabbage flowers in the design.

Jeb hadn't seen Lucy yet, but he had smelled her as soon as they'd arrived.

The pigpen was on the opposite side of the barn. When he exited the far barn door with Sadie, Jeb laid his eyes on the largest pig he'd ever seen. He supposed she was pink under the layer of mud covering her huge body.

Although it was late July and hadn't rained in more than a week, the pigpen was a sea of mud. Little sun reached it due to a dilapidated gray wooden roof protruding from the side of the barn as an over-hang to the pen, as well as several large, gnarled oak trees on the opposite side.

Jeb wasn't sure which smelled worse — the pigpen or Lucy. The latter was busy at the far end of the pen, rooting through the mud with her snout. She looked up when she saw Jeb approach the feeding trough though, and squished her way through the mud toward him as he poured the pan's contents into the trough.

"Here you go, girl," Jeb said, and Lucy responded with a happy grunt.

"Thank you!" Sadie echoed. "That pan is a little heavy for me."

"No problem," Jeb responded. "Be careful; it's slippery."

"I know," Sadie said. "I almost fall every day."

Jeb and Sadie carefully made their way back to the deck under construction. Sadie continued back into the house with her empty pan, while Jeb accepted a sandwich, a bottle of water, and a bag of chips from one of the girls.

Lunch was over quickly. Jeb went back into the tiny basement, checked that water was still flowing easily through the new pipes he'd installed, and cleaned the mess he'd made.

When he was done, he was pleased. He knew he'd made the old farmhouse better for Sadie, her daughter, and her grandkids. Along with the sense of accomplishment, he also had some added confidence. Before he'd started the job he wasn't sure how to do it, but he'd figured it out on his own.

He was glad to get out of the stuffy bathroom, and joined the kids working on building the deck. A slight western breeze slipped through the trees to make the hot sun overhead more bearable.

Rachel, one of the girls on the trip he didn't know well, was bending down and looking at a piece of pressure-treated lumber balanced on a navy blue, plastic milk crate. A circular saw and a tape measure were on the ground beside her.

"Can I help?" Jeb asked her.

"Well, I made my line to cut, but I'm not sure how to run that thing," Rachel said, pointing to the saw with her right sneaker.

"You put your hands here, turn it on, line it up, and saw," Jeb said, demonstrating even though he'd never used a circular saw before either. "How about I hold the board?" he offered.

"That would be good!"

Rachel took another minute to survey the situation, and after a smile of encouragement from Jeb, she lowered clear plastic goggles perched on top of her head, flipped the switch on the saw to power it on, and carefully made a perfect cut.

"I did it!" she said, surprised.

"Yes, you did; great job!" Jeb said, and he meant it.

"Now we just have 29 more to do."

Jeb picked up the next board and put it in place on the milk crate. Rachel got better with each board, and before long they had that assignment completed.

"Now do we have to nail them?" Jeb asked her.

"No, I think other people will do that," Rachel replied. "We just have to take them over to the deck and put them in a pile now."

Caroline was one of the nailers. Jeb thought she might be approaching that job with a little too much enthusiasm, as she was pounding nails so hard she looked like she was mad at someone.

"Gee, take it easy!" Jeb told her.

Caroline just smiled.

Seeing they were free, Phil asked Jeb to measure and cut the lumber they'd need for the steps, and Rachel joined the sanding crew.

"We'll sand it. Another crew will stain and apply polyurethane next week," Phil told them.

Jeb was bone tired when he climbed back on the bus later that day, but it was a 'good' tired. When they returned to school the girls took showers before the boys did, but Jeb took it in stride. He and the others went through the cafeteria line for dinner, and the leaders promised them a trip to the Dairy Queen in town tomorrow night.

This evening they had made a campfire in the school's incinerator next to the parking lot. After a quick devotion session, the workers enjoyed toasting marshmallows as night fell over the tiny town.

Later, Jeb was able to get a quick, icy shower, and he dropped off to sleep promptly after crawling into his sleeping bag. He was so tired, even the snoring of the guy next to him didn't faze him.

The next five days were similar. His group didn't return to Sadie's farm, but tackled other homes needing similar work.

As the week progressed, Jeb discovered he enjoyed working with his hands. He used many tools he'd never used before, and he completed jobs he didn't know he could do. He had new confidence, a sense of accomplishment, and the knowledge he had truly helped people.

There were a few memorable occurrences too. The girls were spooked when wasps poured out of a shed they were cleaning. Rachel almost had a heart attack when she stepped on a snake. Even Jeb did a double take when he bent to put dog food in an outside bowl for a beagle belonging to a home-bound resident, and an opossum looked up at him in anticipation before his bald tail disappeared into the brush.

They were all memories he'd keep with him for the rest of his life.

After Jeb returned home, his father, Mike, was surprised — and pleased — to find his eldest son had a new attitude. Instead of having to nag him to do any chores, Jeb was offering to do some things around the house on his own. He seemed to appreciate what he had now.

Mike had no idea how a trip to Appalachia had changed his son for the better, but he wasn't questioning it. He hoped it would last. He wondered how he could get Jeb's younger brother to go next summer too.

5

Going, Going, Gone!

There was no need for a red circle around July 12 on the calendar posted on the new bulletin board in Minerva Stewart's shiny new kitchen in her shiny new condo. She knew what would happen today. She'd turn 80 years old, and she'd sell most of her worldly possessions at a public auction at her old farmhouse so things would be easier for her only son when she finally died.

That was putting it bluntly, of course, but Minerva had never been one to mince words.

The auction at the family farm would be so big it required two auctioneers working simultaneously. One would concentrate on the farm equipment, the remaining cattle, and the contents of the barn. The other would sell household items out of the big white farmhouse with its huge, welcoming front porch.

It appeared the whole town was planning to attend, as well as folks from the neighboring countryside. Minerva was a member of the Sunnyside Methodist Church, which was handling the concession stands as a fund-raising project. In honor of Minerva's birthday, the ladies of the congregation were bringing cakes so everyone could have a piece of her birthday cake, and they'd have free homemade ice cream to serve on the side.

It was festive, but Minerva didn't feel festive at all as she donned a pair of tan linen slacks, a blue gingham tunic top, and a yellow straw hat. If she were going to be the object of everyone's attention, at least she'd try to look presentable despite the high humidity. She changed her yellow fabric handbag to a blue one better matching her top, making sure her lucky penny was in its place in her wallet.

A crowd was already at the farm when she pulled into the small parking area near the house. Minerva took a red canvas folding chair out of the trunk of her car and opened it under one of the large oak trees in the front yard of the farmhouse, as she knew she wouldn't last long without shade. She popped open a smile on her face like she'd opened the legs of her chair, and tried not to feel overwhelmed.

Once the sale started, Minerva struggled to take it all in stride. She'd already moved most of the things she was keeping to the condo. She couldn't take everything she wanted, of course, since the square footage of the two homes was so different.

She was surprised at how uninterested her son, Michael, was in the family's treasures. He simply didn't want them.

He had assured her she could bid on anything she'd forgotten to take to the condo, but he'd urged her to be frugal because she didn't have room for everything. He stressed a smaller house would be less costly and less of a burden to maintain. Minerva supposed he was right.

She knew most of the people in the crowd. There were a few people she didn't recognize, but it became clear they were pickers from out of town or buyers for antique stores in the city.

Judy and some of her other friends as well as two ladies from the auction house had helped her organize most of the items being sold. The auction-house employees stressed they all follow what they called the 'Ohio' rule — 'Only Handle It Once.'

Minerva was surprised when a few old crocks went for over $100, and she was mystified when someone paid $370 for her Uncle Bill's old rusted bicycle. But as the auction continued, it was hard not to be sad at some of the prices. Her best set of dishes, which served 12, went for only $20. The smallest of its four platters, which Minerva had never used because she thought it was too nice, retailed for over $70.

Minerva's long-time friend, Judy, patted her hand when she noticed a tear slide down Minerva's cheek after a bell from her extensive bell collection garnered a measly $1. Minerva's late husband, Ralph, had paid over $100 for it as his present to her on a previous birthday.

"It'll be OK, Minerva," Judy said. "Try to remember they're just things. Even though you're not keeping the bell, you still have the memory, and that's what's important."

"OK," Minerva said, and swallowed hard.

Minerva took matters into her own hands on a couple occasions, and when the townspeople saw who was bidding, they dropped out. The first time it happened was when a box of old picture frames went up for sale, and Minerva realized her parents' wedding photo was still in the box. She bought her own American flag that used to hang on the porch, as she realized she could hang it on the deck of her new condo. She also bought a gold plaster bust of Abraham Lincoln that Ralph had lugged home one day from someone else's auction.

"What are you going to do with that, Mother?" her son, Michael, asked when he saw the figurine on the ground by the legs of her lawn chair.

"Oh, I just want to keep it; your father said it was valuable," Minerva answered.

"OK." Michael rolled his eyes, but he let the subject drop.

After lunch at the concession stand, Minerva took a little spin around the first floor of the farmhouse. Several women and little Betsy Brown, who was 7, were looking at her doll collection. The dolls were displayed on a large folding table near the fireplace in the living room. They looked like orphans awaiting adoption. Their eyes were glassy, as if the situation was too much for them to comprehend.

"Which one do you like best, Betsy?" Minerva asked the girl.

"That one," Betsy said, pointing to a 1940s Shirley Temple doll. Shirley's trademark curls were under a small Stetson hat, and she was wearing a brown suede cowgirl outfit complete with chaps, a vest, and a small holster holding a tiny silver revolver. The chaps had red accents to match the doll's red shirt and matching neckerchief.

"That's one of my favorites too."

"Maybe I can buy it," Betsy said optimistically with a toss of her curls, which were similar to the doll's. "I have some money."

"How much do you have?"

"$11.43." Betsy patted a small lavender purse sporting a big yellow butterfly. "I got $10 from my grandma for my birthday."

"Well, you never want to spend your last dollar, you know," Minerva advised her.

Betsy wasn't sure what to say in response, but her mother had overheard the remark and chimed in.

"Mrs. Stewart is right," she told Betsy, and after some other small talk they moved on.

Minerva spoke to the auctioneer before she headed back to her lawn chair and steeled herself for Round 2. Benny Norris was one of the two auctioneers. She'd known him for over 30 years.

Eventually the dolls came up for sale. Minerva could see Betsy and her mother across the lawn, watching intently.

Minerva was pleased when her McGuffy Anna doll went for $330. Several others sold in the $200s, and none went for less than $100.

Finally the Shirley Temple cowgirl doll came up for bids.

"What do I hear for this fine Shirley Temple doll? Who will start the bidding?" Benny Norris asked the crowd over his microphone as he and Minerva exchanged nods.

One of the pickers called out "$100," but Benny didn't seem to hear him.

"Betsy, would you like to bid on this doll?" Benny asked, looking at her.

"$10.43!" Betsy called out. She looked at the ground, suddenly afraid.

"I have $10.43!" Benny announced. "Do I hear $11?"

"$11," the picker said. He raised his hand as he did it, but again Benny was deaf towards him.

"Sold to Betsy Brown for $10.43!" Benny declared, hitting his gavel on the stand with a flourish.

Everyone but the picker smiled. Betsy hopped in delight as the doll was passed through the crowd. She hugged it tight when it was placed in her arms.

"Now what will you give for this lovely Raggedy Anne doll?" Benny said, steaming right along.

The picker finally caught on, smiled, and placed a bid on Raggedy Anne.

There were a few snafus. Eleanor Beckenbaugh had to buy back one of her own pie plates that had been returned to Minerva by mistake after a church bake sale. Eleanor recognized it, even though it looked like any other pie plate. Her name was handwritten on a piece of tape on the bottom of the plate, so the cashier didn't accept any money for it when Eleanor explained what happened when she checked out.

Two boys got into a heated tug-of-war over a red metal wagon that had been Michael's when he was their age. Both were put out. One tugged on the handle at the front while the other pulled from the back. Michael ended the disagreement by sitting in the bed of the wagon himself, and told them he'd decided not to sell it after all.

About three-quarters of the way through the auction, Pastor Bachturn borrowed Benny's microphone to address the crowd.

"The Stewart family wants to thank you for attending the sale, and for wishing Minerva the best as she transitions into her new condo," he said. "Change is often not easy, but we're happy Minerva will still be close enough to attend our church.

"Now, did you know today is her 80th birthday?" he asked the crowd. "There is free cake and ice cream at the concession stand for everyone, but first, would you please join me in singing 'Happy Birthday' to her?"

As Minerva blushed, the pastor led the crowd in a rousing rendition of the traditional song. She was touched by their thoughtfulness. Knowing she had good friends throughout the community who cared about her lessened the sting of giving up her treasures.

Later, when all that was left was the cleanup, which was being handled by the church's youth group, Minerva watched Betsy Brown as she clutched her new doll and her mother's hand and headed towards their car.

Yes, they're just things, Minerva reminded herself.

6

Unexpected Blessings

One positive thing about leaving her fiancé at the altar in June and not going on her honeymoon was she had vacation days left, Cassie Hess thought as she sat in the passenger seat of her father's 18-wheeler rolling west on Interstate 70.

She had never been on a trip with her father, Jim, in his truck. She decided to go along this time after she learned he was delivering a load of supplies from their small church in Ohio to victims of a tornado in Oklahoma. Helping others instead of focusing on her own dramas seemed like a positive step. And since she was a nurse, she thought she might be helpful on this trip. Old Doc Burgess had cooperated and given her the new days off with full pay.

The trucking company Jim worked for had been charitable too. The pair had a week before they had to return the truck to the docks so Jim could get loaded for his next regular run.

Cassie hadn't known exactly what to pack, but she was glad she had her sunglasses. Although the sun was behind them, the glare coming through the windshield was intense that hot Monday morning in mid-July. She reached into her handbag for a coated rubber band and some bobby pins and tied her medium-length brown hair into a bun.

The church members had loaded everything yesterday afternoon after church. The trailer was about a third full with bottled water. They also were carrying some tools, two wheelbarrows, cleaning supplies, some non-perishable food, several types of animal feed, many boxes of trash bags, and even diapers. The best clothes left over from the church's last garage sale were in the mix too. Jim also had a small wallet full of gift cards, which he'd been instructed to dole out as he saw fit.

Their initial destination was a small church in Oklahoma coordinating their effort.

Cassie figured her father would broach the subject of her broken engagement sometime during the trip, but so far he'd kept the conversation on safe topics.

The trip was about 800 miles each way. It was already dark after they filled the truck's tank with diesel fuel and pulled into the parking lot of their hotel. The site of the tornado was about 25 miles further west, and they didn't know if fuel would be in short supply in the area or not. They wanted to get a good night's sleep in a regular bed, and proceed to their destination the next morning. They'd sleep in the truck the rest of the trip. The pastor was expecting them around 9 a.m. Tuesday.

When they pulled into the parking lot of the little church the next morning, the pastor came out and greeted them. He had a crew of six men and boys to help unload. Jim was glad to see two of them had hand trucks. The supplies were to go in a metal building out back first, and when it was full they'd pile boxes in the church's hallways. Some of the tornado victims were staying in the church's Fellowship Hall until they could find more permanent lodging.

Jim pointed out several boxes of supplies, two wheelbarrows, and two shovels that were staying in the truck, and the volunteers stuck with the job until it was finished.

Later, the pastor asked Jim and Cassie how long they were going to stay in the area, and what their plans were.

"We're staying through Friday if we can be of help," Jim said. "We thought we'd wing it and see what we could do."

"Bless you," the pastor said. "Most of the town was hit. The worst damage is west of downtown. I'll call the police and tell them to let you into the area. You'll have to give them your names. It's hard to believe, but there are people who will loot in situations like this."

He reached into his pocket, pulled out an old church bulletin, and started to draw a map of the area in the margins until he realized the landmarks he wanted to draw had been blown to smithereens by the tornado.

"Head west; you can't miss it," he said, and added, "Stop by the kitchen in Fellowship Hall and pick up bagged lunches before you go."

The effects of the tornado were worse than what TV portrayed. After going through the police checkpoint, Cassie and Jim were struck by the randomness and the enormity of the disaster. They also couldn't help but wonder how they'd react if put in this situation. As far as they could see, everything was shattered, smashed, and soaked. Clumps of pink insulation dotted the debris, looking like piles of cotton candy.

They passed 18 utility trucks. Workers were picking up downed lines, setting new poles, and trying to get service restored. The dangers of downed electric lines and gas line breaks weren't lost on Cassie or Jim.

A young woman about Cassie's age was working alone in one area, going through what was left of her house, and putting the debris in piles. Jim pulled the 18-wheeler off the side of the road and they walked over to her and introduced themselves. She was slim and dressed in jeans and a T-shirt. A few strands of her short blonde hair peeked out under an old John Deere cap.

"Hi! I'm Emma, and this used to be our house," she told them. "My husband works as a private contractor in the Mideast and can't get back here yet, so it's just me and our two kids. The kids are in Tulsa, staying with my mom."

"You don't have anyone else helping you?" Jim asked.

"It's just me for now," Emma admitted. "Everyone else I know in the area is busy with their own houses. My other relatives are too far away."

As they talked, Jim and Cassie learned Emma and her boys had heard the tornado sirens in time and escaped injury by huddling in their basement. Emma said more than once how grateful she was their ranch house came with a basement, instead of being built on a concrete slab.

It was late in the season for a tornado, but it had been a big one. "We never saw it; we just heard it," Emma related. "We could hear things breaking and cracking, and in less than a minute we lost everything," she said sadly. "But we're lucky to be alive. Several people weren't so lucky."

"We'll give you a hand for awhile," Jim said. He and Cassie headed back to the truck for their wheelbarrows, gloves, sunblock, garbage bags, and a couple of bottles of water.

"I'm much obliged," Emma said with her slight Southern drawl.

There wasn't much to salvage, but they kept working. Emma wiped away tears from her deep-blue eyes several times.

Jim and Cassie learned she was staying in a shelter the Red Cross had set up in the local high school.

"I hadn't been in there since graduation day," Emma noted. "I never thought I'd be homeless and sleeping on a cot in the gym."

Even the trees framing the property were broken and provided no shade, so the trio took breaks regularly to pace themselves. Emma had made makeshift seats out of a broken toy box and a metal washtub that had escaped unscathed. A tarp hung over some rope stretching between two beams that used to be part of her house. It provided some shade over the seating area.

They ate a late lunch of sandwiches, chips, and water under the tarp. Emma had packed her lunch in the school cafeteria.

As they worked that afternoon, Jim and Cassie would show objects to Emma when they came upon something that might be salvageable. She kept some things and nodded her head sadly at others. The piles of debris grew steadily.

Emma found the remnants of her wedding album around 3 p.m. The album was ruined, but she put it in a small plastic bag anyway. She was hunting for baby photos of her sons, but so far she was coming up empty.

At one point Cassie screamed when she moved a piece of drywall and a raccoon scampered out. They also saw a rabbit, and a golden eagle soared ahead.

"Tornadoes are hard on the wildlife too," Jim noted.

Late that afternoon a wiry terrier appeared out of nowhere, bounced over to Jim, and lay a dirty pink rubber ball by his feet.

"Where did you come from?" Jim asked him, but the dog wasn't talking.

"Did we leave all the dog food at the church, or do we still have some in the trailer?" Jim asked Cassie.

"I don't know; I'll go look," Cassie replied. She needed a bathroom break anyway, and no one would see her if she relieved herself behind the truck.

She eventually returned with bottles of water and a small bag of potato chips. Emma overturned the lid of what was left of her best saucepan to create a makeshift bowl, and they laid out the chips and poured water into the lid for the dog.

He wolfed it down like he hadn't eaten in days, which they imagined was likely. He had no collar, so of course there were no tags.

The dog liked Jim immediately. He wagged his tail and looked at him so expectantly after dropping his ball at Jim's feet that Jim played along.

"How long are you going to work today, and how are you getting back to the school?" Cassie asked Emma at one point.

"A van will pick me up unless I walk back myself," she said. "I've had about all I can take for today. I'm supposed to have a rental car from my insurance company waiting for me at the airport in Oklahoma City, but I haven't been able to get there to pick it up yet," she added. "I'm one of the lucky ones; I have my driver's license. I was able to grab my purse before I headed for the basement, and my cell phone was in my purse too. I've been able to use a charger belonging to a lady at the school."

"We could give her a ride, couldn't we, Dad?" Cassie asked, and that's how the three of them called it quits for the day, climbed into the cab of the truck, and headed for the Oklahoma City Airport. The dog wouldn't leave Jim alone, so he picked him up and he went along too, taking turns riding on each young woman's lap despite the fact he needed a bath.

During the ride, the new friends continued to chat.

"Since he's overseas, my husband's paycheck will still be coming,"

Emma confided. "I'm worried most about my kids. Mom said Jason, who is my youngest, couldn't stop crying the other night when a thunderstorm blew up. John, my oldest, has been entirely too quiet. Mom is trying to find a counselor for them."

"This happened quickly, but it's not going to get back to normal anytime soon," Cassie noted wisely. "You're going to have to work at not getting burned out."

"I know," Emma agreed. "My 'to-do' list is incredible, when I can even find paper to write it down."

She looked at the passing scenery. "Last week I was wondering how I was going to find time to wash my windows. Now I don't have any windows, and I'm just trying not to get cut on all the broken glass. But I know I'm lucky," she added quickly. "We could have been killed, but we're OK. That's what matters."

Jim admired her attitude and told her so. "The only thing you can do is clean it all up and focus on the future," he told her.

"I know, but this is a heck of a way to convince my husband to get me new granite countertops for our kitchen."

They got the rental car with a minimum of fuss, which surprised them. Cassie rode with Emma on the way back to the school in their mini-convoy. They stopped at a truck stop for a late dinner and some extra supplies, including a bag of dog food. "Twister," which was the name Jim had given the dog, devoured the portion they gave him at the truck stop before getting on the road again, and he slept with Jim in the lower bunk of the truck's cab that night. Cassie took the top bunk.

Jim and Cassie were digging through the rubble of Emma's house when she arrived the next morning in her rental car.

"I don't know what I would do without you!" Emma told them.

"Well, we're only here for a couple more days," Jim reminded her. "But we'll do what we can."

"You've already done so much." Emma picked up a shovel and started to work.

Twister was keeping close to Jim.

"Do you know whose dog this is?" Jim asked Emma.

"No idea; I don't remember ever seeing him before."

They continued the backbreaking work, again reminding themselves to apply sunblock, drink water, and take breaks periodically.

Certain things they found amazed them. Although the house was now rubble, there were green beans needing to be picked in what was left of Emma's garden.

"Let the rabbits have them; I don't have any way to put beans up this year," Emma said. "All my canning jars are smashed."

That afternoon, a white pickup headed their way at speed.

"It's Jerry Barnes. He lives down the road," Emma said.

"I need help! Joey fell and I think he broke his leg!" Jerry yelled through the window. "I don't have phone service. The battery died a long time ago, and I don't know where the charger is."

"We'll be right there; Cassie is a nurse, and we have cell phones!" Emma replied, and she, Cassie, and Jim dropped everything and ran for Emma's rental car. Emma threw the keys to Jim so he drove, and followed Jerry's pickup down the lane. Cassie dialed 9-1-1 and handed the phone to Emma so she could provide directions as soon as the dispatcher answered.

There was no doubt Jerry's son Joey had broken his leg. Cassie could see part of the bone protruding from a long rip in the teenager's jeans. He'd been moving some boards around in a loft in one of their damaged outbuildings, slipped, and fell.

"Stay as still as possible," she told him, and asked for a blanket to try to keep him warm. They couldn't find one, but Cassie kept Joey talking and still and monitored his pulse until the ambulance arrived and the EMTs took over.

On Thursday morning they had a visit from another neighbor, Carol Hall, who looked to be in her sixties. She clutched a small photo of two young boys in her right hand.

"Aren't these your two?" she asked Emma, who was overjoyed to receive the photo she'd taken before they climbed onto the bus on the first day of school last September.

"I found it stuck in what's left of my apple tree, and I live at least a mile away," Carol told them.

That afternoon Cassie and Jim stopped at the local animal shelter with Twister. No one had reported a similar dog as missing, and the staff couldn't find a microchip on him. Twister got a bath and a quick medical examination. One of the shelter workers also helped them fill out a form and took a photo of the dog, along with Jim's contact information. Jim had already decided to take Twister back to Ohio with him, but if he belonged to somebody, he'd return him.

The yard around what had been Emma's house at least looked more orderly on the last day Jim and Cassie worked with her.

"Can't you stay until the bulldozers and dump trucks come?" Emma asked.

"We have to get back," Jim said. "I have a couple gift cards from my wife's church to help you out a little, and I hope you can stay positive as you continue to work through this."

"I can't thank you enough," Emma replied. "I've learned sometimes there's no other option but to hold on, get busy, and stay positive," she said sincerely. "But unexpected blessings like total strangers being a big help can come out of a disaster too."

7

Doreen's Day Off

"But I don't want to go to summer school!"

Doreen squirmed in her seat, folded her arms across her chest, and stuck her lower lip out like she was 6 instead of 22.

The black, industrial clock on the wall ticked loudly and a fly buzzed against a screen in a window of the rec room at the East Side House of Hope that Saturday morning in late June. The carcasses of four other flies lay beneath the buzzing one, caught between the panes of glass where they had died. Although the oppressive humidity of summer was still a month away, it was already hot in the homeless shelter, which had always had poor circulation.

Doreen rose, lifted the window and the screen, and set the fly free.

"I'm tired!" she declared sadly. "I'm not good at anything, and I'll never be able to get a job."

"Yes, you will," Cheryl assured her quickly. "Instead of thinking about what you can't do, we're going to concentrate on what you can do," she added, running her slender fingers through her short, black hair. "We're going to get you the training you need, and you'll be on your way."

Doreen and her 5-year-old son, Davey, had arrived at the shelter's front door last November after being on the streets for about seven months.

Cheryl's first encounter with the residents and staff of the East Side House of Hope had been a month later, when she dropped off a Christmas donation of a carload of socks for her friend Mary Jean, who had been a volunteer there for many years. Cheryl had made a New Year's resolution to become more active in the community, and she started serving as a volunteer there later in January.

At first she organized crafts and played board games with the residents, but she'd struck up an easy friendship with Doreen, who was close to her own age. Cheryl wasn't qualified to work on Doreen's "case," but she had been more than willing to accept the request of the shelter's director, Burt Baxter, to become Doreen's personal advocate. It was a fancy term for friend.

Doreen had been a good sport about everything, so Cheryl was surprised she was resisting the shelter's offer for training now.

Mr. Baxter had enrolled Doreen in a substance-abuse class almost immediately. After about a month of being ill with flu-link symptoms, vomiting regularly, and living with a severe case of the shakes, Doreen had stayed relatively clean.

He enrolled her in Alcoholic Anonymous classes too. Cheryl knew Doreen had at least two flasks hidden at the shelter, but she and Doreen's primary therapist, Lillian Hall, were confident she was making headway.

Cheryl had been shocked to discover how easy it was for people who had no home and little money to still get drugs and alcohol to feed their addictions.

She didn't want to know how low Doreen stooped in pursuit of her bad habits.

Mr. Baxter, Lillian, and Cheryl all knew Davey was their secret weapon in working with Doreen. She wouldn't talk about her child's father, but it was obvious she wanted to be a better mother than her own had been.

"When you were a little girl, what did you want to be when you grew up?" Cheryl pressed her now.

"A nurse, but I get queasy at the sight of blood," Doreen said. "Then I wanted to be a beautician, but people don't seem to appreciate my excellent taste."

Cheryl smiled. At the moment Doreen was wearing leopard-spotted leggings and a chartreuse green T-shirt. Her hair color was growing out, but it was still primarily neon pink. She always painted her enormously long fingernails in wild colors. Today they were bright orange with paste-on rhinestone dots, although some of the dots had already fallen off. A dangling pair of large, red plastic earrings spilled like twin streams of molten lava onto her shoulders.

"What about now?" Cheryl prodded.

"I still think I could be a good beautician, and maybe I could be a cop," Doreen replied. "You know, if you can't beat 'em, join 'em."

Cheryl smiled. She didn't think Doreen would be particularly good as a beautician because her style was so different than the general public's. The idea of her working in law enforcement was a stretch too, but she was determined to make something work.

"Why would you like to become a police officer?"

"Oh, I don't know. They get to solve crimes, and I like mysteries. And they get to eat donuts whenever they want."

"They also have a lot of paperwork, they work long hours, sometimes their days are boring, and they could be shot and killed at any time," Cheryl pointed out.

"Boy, you're a real downer," Doreen said, but it didn't seem to deter her. "I don't want to go to summer school," she insisted. "I've been through a lot this year, and I want some time off. You people expect a lot."

That was true. Mr. Baxter ran a tight ship, and the residents of the East Side House of Hope were required to do their share of physical work. Besides taking care of her son, going to classes, and writing in a journal daily, Doreen had pitched in. She babysat the children of other mothers, helped with meals and cleanup duties in the kitchen, and helped with the center's laundry. She had free time for TV, board games, crafts, and the occasional basketball game, but she had been working hard to turn her life around for herself and her son.

"We're building on your strengths, setting some achievable goals, and taking it one day at a time," Cheryl reminded her, reciting the phrase she spouted to Doreen often.

"Well, I don't know what kind of job I can get," Doreen repeated, doubtfully. "I didn't finish high school."

"You can earn your high school diploma through the shelter."

"It would be good to finally find myself," Doreen admitted.

"I've learned you create yourself more than find yourself in life," Cheryl replied.

"You have an answer for everything, don't you?" Doreen said, looking at her sideways.

"Hardly," Cheryl grinned. "I don't even get along with my own mother very well. But you think about what kind of a career you want to create. And in the meantime, I think maybe what you need the most right now is a day off."

"That would be great!" Doreen said enthusiastically. "Can we go to one of the bars around here?" she added, not thinking.

"Well, no, but we can find something else fun to do," Cheryl replied. "Go see if one of the other mothers will look after Davey. I don't have much money on me but I have the afternoon free, so let's get out of here right after lunch!"

About an hour later Doreen and Cheryl were on their way in Cheryl's little blue hatchback.

"Where are we going?" Doreen asked.

"That's a surprise," Cheryl said and headed south on the interstate. She turned off at the exit of a small town about 20 minutes later, and parked in a parking lot downtown.

"This place always makes me feel better," she told Doreen, who followed her into a small pavilion. In front of them was a full-sized, antique merry-go-round, with carved wooden horses, tigers, lions, bears, and even ostriches mounted on its circular floor. Hundreds of small yellow light bulbs flashed, and calliope music blasted out of the merry-go-round's sound system. Children and adults flashed by as it turned, while others stood in line for the next ride.

Doreen's feet were planted in the same spot they'd been in when she first saw the merry-go-round. She looked like a deer caught in headlights.

"I've never been on a merry-go-round before," she told Cheryl. "I ain't even seen a real merry-go-round before."

"Well, there's a first time for everything," Cheryl said. "I'll get the tickets, and you figure out what you want to ride first!"

When Cheryl returned, Doreen was already at the back of the line.

"We should have brought Davey," Doreen said.

"There will be another time for that; this is just a girls' day off," Cheryl told her.

When the merry-go-round stopped, they had to walk to the other side before they found a black horse and an orange tiger available for riders. Cheryl climbed aboard the tiger, while Doreen clambered onto the horse. Once she was settled, she looped the handles of her pocketbook over its head.

"I've never ridden a horse before," Doreen told her.

"Hold on, because this merry-go-round goes faster than you think," Cheryl advised her.

In less than a minute the lights flashed, the volume of the music increased, and the merry-go-round began to spin. Doreen smiled widely as her horse sank and rose, mimicking a horse cantering.

"This is fun!" she proclaimed to Cheryl as the walls of the building went by in a blur. She wondered what her friends on the street would think of her if they saw her now. "It's not my usual kind of fun, but it's still fun!" she repeated.

"I know!" Cheryl said.

When that ride was over, they moved on to two different animals for the next round, as Cheryl had purchased multiple tickets. They each had four rides that afternoon.

"Now what?" Doreen asked as they walked back to the car, trying not to think about how good a swig from the flask deep in her purse would taste.

"Retail therapy!" Cheryl announced.

"I like the sound of that!" Doreen said, and a few minutes later they arrived at the town's Goodwill store.

"I've heard this store gets a lot more higher-end donations than the one closest to the shelter does, so let's check it out," Cheryl said. "I have enough money that we each can spend $20."

"Thanks!" Doreen said. She couldn't remember the last time she'd gone shopping.

The two young women spent the next two hours looking for treasures among the women's racks of clothes. They tried things on, and gave honest opinions about what worked and what didn't. Cheryl carefully suggested Doreen look for some clothes appropriate for school, and was pleased when Doreen didn't give her a look.

The store had exchanged most of its winter clothes for summer clothes, but there were still some sweaters out that had been marked down drastically. When they finally headed to the checkout line, Cheryl had three new turtlenecks, a blue blazer, a scarf, and a pair of reading glasses.

Doreen chose a pair of jeans, a tie-dyed T-shirt, two pairs of black slacks, two tame-for-her blouses, a bulky red sweater, and a lilac shoulder bag with purple fringe.

"Thank you!" Doreen remembered to say as they loaded the bags in the car. "Now what?"

"We have time for one more stop, I think," Cheryl said, and a few minutes later she pulled into the parking lot of a roadside soft ice cream store, The Hungry Cow.

"They always have at least three flavors — vanilla, chocolate and the flavor of the month," Cheryl advised.

The flavor of the month turned out to be strawberry, but both women chose two scoops of chocolate. Cheryl had hers in a dish, while Doreen chose a waffle cone.

They ate at a picnic table next to the stand. As the first bites of soft ice cream slipped down their throats, both women sighed.

"This hits the spot!" Doreen declared. Cheryl nodded, and they continued to enjoy their dessert in companionable silence.

A minute later, Doreen spoke. She was becoming as corny as her new friends.

"Knock, knock!" she said.

"Who's there?" Cheryl played along.

"Ice cream."

"Ice cream who?"

"I'll scream if you make me go to summer school," Doreen giggled, and they smiled.

"Very funny," Cheryl said. "But you know it's for the best."

"I know," Doreen said. "But would you please see if there are any programs I can get into that would lead to a job as a cop or a detective?"

"I'll see what I can do," Cheryl agreed, and they finished their ice cream with Doreen's career goals established.

8

Independence Day

As he drove to the Fourth of July concert on the outskirts of a neighboring city, Rick Hunley could tell the brunette beside him in his SUV was excited. She sat erectly in her seat, fidgeted a little, and couldn't stop smiling.

Since it was their first date, Rick wasn't sure if Kate Martin was just happy to have the holiday off, if she was thrilled for the chance to see one of her favorite country stars perform live, or if she was pleased to be going out with him. He hoped it was a combination of all three.

"Thanks again for inviting me; I love Alan Connor!" she told him as she hooked a lock of her medium-length hair over her left ear.

Kate was about five feet eight, while Rick was every bit of six feet. Kate wore a turquoise tunic top that brought out her green eyes, jeans, and tan cowboy boots. Her outfit had a definite Western twang, primarily due to the boots, her turquoise earrings, matching cuff bracelet, and leather-tooled purse.

Rick had met her at the feed store where he bought supplies for his small farm in central Pennsylvania. She was a clerk there. She'd come to town a couple of years ago to care for an elderly aunt, and stayed when the aunt died and left her rambling Victorian house and the rest of her estate to Kate in her will.

Rick hadn't considered asking Kate out before, but when a high-school friend who was in Alan Connor's band sent him two free tickets to the concert, he made the offer. He figured the odds were good she'd like the show. She had hung an Alan Connor poster near the feed store's cash register, and she always had the store's radio set to a country station.

Rick didn't date much. His last serious relationship had broken his heart three years ago, around the same time Kate had arrived in town. He'd dated Becky Grove exclusively for two years. He was blindsided when she abruptly quit her job as a music teacher at the local middle school, and left for Los Angeles a week later to pursue an acting career.

Rick had thought Becky was 'the one,' and he'd been more than hurt. Their last encounter had been rocky. He hadn't heard from her again, although he still thought about her daily. He had replayed the relationship over and over in his mind so many times it had almost grown into an obsession, but three years later he still had no answers.

The concert was being held on the edge of a large fairgrounds. They waited in line to park, and were directed to a large field some distance from the temporary stage they could see ahead of them. Parking attendants wearing vinyl, florescent-orange vests directed the traffic into long rows of vehicles, but there weren't any lines on the ground to separate the rows, or any lights like in traditional parking lots.

After they parked, Rick pulled two lawn chairs, a small picnic basket, and a small cooler from the rear of the SUV, and he and Kate followed the crowd towards the stage. They found a good spot in the middle of the audience, planted their chairs, visited the mobile restrooms, and were settled for the evening a full 30 minutes before the concert's starting time. It was an hour before sunset and it was still hot, but they used that opportunity to eat the dinner Rick had purchased at a popular deli in their town: fried chicken, rolls, potato chips, and pickles. He also provided soft drinks and beer in the small, soft-plastic cooler.

As they ate, they continued to get acquainted. Rick learned Kate's closest relative had been that aunt. She learned his elderly parents were still living and he had a sister, but his two brothers had died in separate traffic accidents several years apart at Christmastime.

Kate already knew Rick was an electrician, but he was surprised to learn she had a veterinary technician degree. She owned two Quarter horses she boarded at a local farm, and she barrel-raced one in regional and selected national events.

Eventually the opening act came on the stage. The large crowd listened politely. The lead singer wasn't bad, but the crowd had come for Alan Connor, and that's whom they wanted to see.

When the star finally came on stage, he didn't disappoint. Rick pointed out his high-school friend playing guitar in the band, and he smiled and joined along when Kate clapped to the up-tempo songs. The crowd seemed to be as enamored as she was, and she seemed to be on Cloud 9.

"This is great!" Kate confirmed at intermission when they could talk without shouting.

"I'm glad you're having fun; I am too!" Rick said. "I'm not a big country music fan, but even I know some of these songs."

"What kind of music do you like?"

"Rock, but don't hold that against me." Rick stroked his chin under his short, neatly trimmed brown beard.

"I won't!"

More casual conversation followed. The stage lights blinked and an announcement was made saying the show would resume in five minutes.

About 15 minutes into the second half of the show, Rick's world was rocked. Alan invited a random fan onto the stage to sing one of his hits with him, and that fan turned out to be Becky Grove.

She was more tanned than he remembered, but just as beautiful. The crowd, unaware of her background in music and acting, applauded when she confidently sang along with the star. When the song was over Alan presented her with a video of their performance, and an usher helped her back to her seat as a spotlight followed along.

Rick couldn't keep his eyes off her. All his emotions flooded back as strong as ever.

"I'm sorry, Kate; that's an old friend I have to see," he mumbled to his date as he stood and headed towards Becky, unable and unwilling to stop.

When he reached her in the audience, he realized she was with a group of girlfriends. She was as shocked to see him as he'd been to see her.

"Rick!" she said. "What a surprise! How are you?"

The concert was continuing, but luckily it was a slow song, and they could each hear the other over the music.

"I'm fine," he said automatically, and without thinking blurted out, "As fine as I can be without you. Why did you leave me?"

Becky shook her head and looked at her sandals.

"It was nothing personal; I just had to follow my dreams," she replied, sinking into her lawn chair. Rick dropped on his haunches beside her so he wouldn't be standing in front of the audience.

"Nothing personal?" Rick repeated, dumbfounded. "It was personal to me. I loved you."

"I know, and I'm sorry."

Rick regrouped, and he had more questions. "Are you back in the area? Are you seeing anyone? May I call you?"

"Oh, Rick." Becky reached for her bag. "Here's my card, but I'm only in town for the holiday. I'm going back to LA tomorrow."

Rick took the card and carefully put it into his pocket. "What we had was special. I think we deserve a second chance."

"How are you, really?" Becky repeated, ignoring the comment. "I heard your brother Jeff died last Christmas. I'm sorry."

"Yes; it was tough," Rick admitted.

"Are you still working as an electrician?" she ventured.

There was something in the way she said 'electrician' Rick didn't like, but he answered without hesitation. "Yes; it's honest work."

"I see," Becky said dismissively. "We can't talk during the concert; you better go back to your seat."

"I guess you're right." Rick began to rise, but he caught her face in both hands and smothered her mouth in one powerful, passionate kiss. Becky was caught off guard, but in a few seconds she opened her lips in response.

When their lips parted, Rick looked into her eyes with three years of pent-up longing. She looked at him questioningly, but a few seconds later a loud clap of thunder punctured the music, and the crowd was pelted with large drops of rain. No announcement was made, but in an instant everyone realized the rest of the concert and the fireworks finale were canceled.

"We need to go!" Becky yelled, and in a flurry of motions she and her girlfriends gathered their belongings and dashed towards the parking area, leaving Rick standing alone in the rain.

He stood for a few minutes, oblivious to everything, deep in thought. When he broke out of his daze, he was being pelted with rain and he was alone in a field that was beginning to turn muddy.

"Kate!" he remembered.

He walked back to where they had been sitting, but there were no signs of Kate, the lawn chairs, the picnic basket, or the cooler.

Rick sloshed his way towards the pitch-black field where his SUV was parked, but with no lights, lines, or landmarks to guide him, an enormous number of cars, and the driving rain, he wasn't sure where his car was. Water streamed everywhere and the wind increased, making visibility even harder. He tried not to panic, but he honestly couldn't find his car. He squinted to try to keep some of the rain out of his eyes, but it was no use. He reached into his right front jeans pocket and pulled out his key ring holding his car keys and remote, but when he pressed the remote's button to make the vehicle's head-lights flash and the horn sound, he still couldn't locate his car.

To make matters worse, there was no orderly exit of the crowd. Cars were cutting each other off left and right like a stampede as fans fled the area, realizing their chances of getting mired in the mud increased with every moment they tarried. Their cars' headlights did illuminate some of the area, but the result was more spooky than helpful.

When Rick finally spotted his SUV and squished his way towards it, Kate and his lawn chairs were leaning against the passenger side's front fender, and the picnic basket and cooler were on the car's roof. It was still raining, and it was obvious Kate had fallen on her walk back to the car. Besides being soaked, streaks of mud were splattered on her tunic, her hair was flat and dripping water, and her jeans and boots were muddy. Her left earring was missing, and her teeth were chattering. Rick wondered if that was from the cold or anger.

"Let me in, please," was all she said when he approached.

"I'm sorry; I couldn't find the car," Rick said as he pushed the button on the remote. All four doors unlocked immediately.

Kate opened the front passenger door, climbed inside, and plopped onto the seat with a sigh.

After depositing the lawn chairs and the other supplies in the back of the SUV, Rick produced a roll of paper towels and handed it to Kate when he joined her inside the car.

"I had trouble finding it too, and I fell in the mud and twisted my ankle," she said as she unwound a few towels and wiped away some of the mud. "Don't say anything about your upholstery if you want to live," she warned. "And I saw you kissing that girl."

"I'm sorry, Kate," Rick repeated, but offered no other explanation. Noticing a clump of mud stuck to Kate's left temple, he reached over, wiped it away, rolled down his window, and dropped it outside.

They sat in silence as Rick turned the key in the ignition, turned on the headlights, and followed the few remaining cars towards the exit.

"Well, the first half of the concert was great!" Rick said, hoping to lighten the mood.

"Yes, it was," Kate agreed, but said nothing more.

"Should we stop at a clinic somewhere to have them look at your ankle?"

"It's just twisted; I'll live." Kate looked straight ahead. "I just want to go home so I can get out of these clothes and get a hot shower."

"Yes, that sounds good to me too," Rick admitted. He turned on the car's radio and dialed in a country station. Ironically, Alan Connor's latest hit poured from the car's speakers.

Rick apologized again when they reached Kate's house. It had finally stopped raining, but the storm hadn't made a dent in the high humidity.

Rick jumped out first, ran to the passenger-side door, and helped Kate out. She took his hand, and they walked together to her front door, Kate limping slightly. Rick took the house key from her, turned the lock, and opened the door.

"I'll be fine," she said as she went through the door. Turning towards him to retrieve her key, she added, "Thank you for a memorable evening. I enjoyed the concert."

"Thanks for going along," Rick replied, and he returned to his car, turned around in her driveway, and headed home.

The next day on his lunch hour, he made a call to a local florist and ordered a large, summer bouquet of flowers. He'd known the lady who answered the phone, Mary McCracken, for years. He had an account there, and he knew Mary would keep his personal business confidential.

"Should I make a big bouquet of say sunflowers, daisies, and assorted mums, or do you have a specific request?" she asked.

"That sounds good," Rick replied.

"What kind of a card?"

"Just a general card."

"What goes on the card?" Mary waited, her pen poised, to record his response.

"'Can we try again?' and my first name," Rick replied.

Mary dutifully wrote the message.

"And who are we delivering these to?"

Several seconds passed. Rick swallowed hard. "Kate Martin, over at the feed store," he said with conviction, smiling with the knowledge he was finally ready for a fresh start.

9

Play Ball!

Maria Ricardo; her son, Juan; daughter-in-law, Sophia; and Juan and Sophia's daughters, Martina and Lola, were pleased with their seats at Victory Field in downtown Indianapolis to watch the Indianapolis Indians take on the Columbus Clippers that Tuesday night in early August. They were sitting near third base, six rows from the field.

The tickets had been a gift from a long-time family friend, Eduardo Sanchez, who was the starting pitcher for the Indians. He'd been in the same high-school class in Texas as another of Maria's sons, Sebastian, who was serving with the U.S. Army in Afghanistan.

The Romantics' "What I Like About You" was playing on the PA system, and some young girls to Maria's right were bouncing along with the music. The ground crew was spraying the field with water even though it had rained earlier, which had delayed things by at least 25 minutes but done nothing to break the humidity. A cotton-candy vendor worked the crowd, offering pink and blue cotton candy. Maria watched one kid flag him down and buy some of the blue variety. The kid ate a few bites, closed the plastic bag, and chewed on the corner of it.

"These are great seats!" Sophia said.

"Yes!" Maria agreed. "The only thing missing is Sebastian. He loves baseball, and he would have been pleased to see Eduardo pitch."

Sophia nodded. Maria didn't want to spoil the evening, but she was worried about Seb. She knew he had been assigned to go on a dangerous mission overseas, and she hadn't heard from him in months. He had told her not to worry, but it wasn't like him to not keep in touch.

Although the game hadn't started, a boy in the row in front of them was eating his second chocolate ice cream cone. His dad was enjoying some French fries smothered in cheese, and his mom was preoccupied with a plastic tray filled with nachos and cheese sauce. She was wearing a white tank top over a bright green sports bra, and she had a big anchor tattoo on her left arm, like a sailor would have. A beer was in her seat's cup holder. She had dyed red hair, and her sunglasses were perched on the top of her head, like a bird sitting in a bush. Maria felt a little conservative in comparison, as she was wearing capri-length jeans, sneakers, and a red tunic top that complimented her short, coal-black hair.

Maria enjoyed people watching. Some of the fathers in the crowd were explaining the game to their sons. Other people were engrossed with their scorecards and programs. Still others were on their cell phones. Some of them were taking selfies and posting them to social media. The tangy smell of ketchup mingled with beer hops and heavily salted popcorn filled the air.

Ushers wearing yellow and orange Hawaiian shirts escorted some game-goers to their seats. Maria studied one of these ushers, who was a teenage girl with brown hair, except for the part that was in a ponytail, which was dyed Kelly green. She was wearing big brown-plastic glasses that had been popular in the seventies, and were popular once again.

There were a couple empty seats to Maria's left, next to the aisle. As Maria watched an Indians player toss a baseball to a kid in the first row, she didn't notice the team's mascot, Rowdie the Bear, had slipped into the aisle to her left, accompanied by a teenage girl named Sherry, who was carrying a wireless microphone. Rowdie towered over the girl, who was wearing a red shirt and shorts in the pattern of a tapestry rug, complete with white fringe on the bottom hems of both legs. She also wore brown cowboy boots and a wide smile.

"Maria Ricardo?" she asked.

"Yes," Maria answered, surprised.

"You're sitting in Row F, Seat 12, and the person in that seat tonight wins the opportunity to go out on the field and say 'Play Ball!' after the national anthem!" Sherry told her excitedly.

"Me? Oh no, I can't do that; pick Sophia," Maria said.

"No, you can do it," Sophia said.

Maria looked at their expectant faces and relented. "That's all I have to do? Just say 'Play ball?'" she asked.

When assured that was all, she went along with it.

"We're going to go into the dugout now, and we'll come out onto the field when it's time," Sherry told her, as Rowdie clapped in excitement.

"Now? Oh! OK." Maria gave Sophia her purse, and hesitantly followed Rowdie and Sherry up the stairs, down another aisle, and into the dugout.

At least this would give her a chance to thank Eduardo for the tickets, and to wish him luck. She found him with no problem, as he came over to her as soon as he saw her. He had a signed Indians baseball cap for her, as well as a hug.

"Thank you," Maria said, touched. "This is so nice of you."

Sherry offered her a seat in a metal folding chair, and told her it wouldn't be long until they had the opening ceremonies and played the national anthem. She would come and get her when it was time, and Maria would go out onto the field and say 'Play ball' into Sherry's wireless microphone.

"Easy peasy," Maria said, getting into the spirit.

As she sat in the dugout, Maria had a great view of the bright green field, mowed in a crosshatch pattern. The field was lit with eight big lights, each holding 19 to 32 light bulbs. The J.W. Marriott hotel, a huge mountain of contemporary blue glass, was to the left of the outfield, and Lucas Oil Stadium could be seen to the right. Four flags were at the center of the outfield. The American flag was the biggest, and in the center. The Indiana state flag, a POW/MIA flag, and a flag for the city of Indianapolis flanked it.

Maria tried not to think about the POW/MIA flag. She hadn't heard from Seb since late April. He'd warned her he might not be in touch for a while. Everyone told her "No news is good news," but she still worried.

Eventually the players lined up in various rows throughout the field for the national anthem, with their caps over their hearts. The Indians were wearing white uniforms with red lettering, while the Columbus Clippers wore gray uniforms with blue lettering.

Sherry motioned to Maria to stand next to her on the field, and Maria complied.

The PA announcer asked everyone to rise and remove their hats for the playing of the national anthem, and Maria obediently took off her new Indians cap. The big screen had a video of an American flag waving. A trumpet player from the Indianapolis Symphony Orchestra stood next to Sherry and Maria and played a rousing rendition of the national anthem directly into Sherry's wireless microphone.

About halfway through the song, Maria and the rest of the crowd noticed a parachutist with an American flag circling down to the field beneath a baby-blue parachute. Maria hadn't noticed the small plane he had jumped out of, but like everyone else she watched him twirl his way to earth like a dry, papery maple-seed helicopter drifting to the ground.

As he approached, she could see him work cords on his right and left as he maneuvered ever closer to the field. With perfect timing, he landed on second base as the trumpeter sounded the final notes of the anthem.

Maria knew her part was coming, but Sherry said it would be a minute until the parachutist finished. The trumpeter made his way back to the dugout, and the players took their places as the parachutist stuffed his parachute into a ball and hurried towards them.

There was something about his walk that seemed familiar to Maria. Her eyes grew wide as she realized the parachutist was Seb! She shook her head, began to cry, and ran toward him as fast as she could run on her short legs.

He had been watching her all along, and ran towards her too. When they met near the pitcher's mound, he dropped all his equipment and hugged her fiercely, picking her up in the process.

Rowdie was so excited that he did a handstand.

Sherry came on the PA but Maria never heard her, nor realized the reunion was being filmed and shown on the stadium's big screen.

"The Indianapolis Indians are proud to welcome Specialist Sebastian Ricardo of the U.S. Army's Special Operations Aviation Command, who is coming home after a dangerous mission in

Afghanistan," Sherry told the crowd. "Here to meet him is his mother, Maria, who lives in Indianapolis."

The crowd cheered and gave them a standing ovation. Many people had tears in their eyes, but neither Seb nor Maria saw them through their own tears.

"Hi, Mom; I'm home for good," Seb told her quietly.

"You didn't re-enlist?"

"No; I'm going to start job-hunting in Indy on Monday."

Eduardo, who had been instrumental in arranging the whole surprise, shook hands with his boyhood friend, and Maria and Seb continued to walk arm in arm towards the dugout.

There was more, however.

The PA announcer came over the air again.

"To thank Seb for his service, he and his mother will receive a week-long Caribbean cruise courtesy of Empress Cruise Lines," the announcer said.

"A cruise? Wow! I've never been on a cruise!" Maria exclaimed.

"Hey, are you forgetting something?" Sherry asked them as they drew near her.

Maria and Seb laughed, simultaneously yelled "Play ball!" into Sherry's microphone, and the crowd roared its approval. Afterward Maria and Seb were escorted to the grandstands to join the other members of their family. Juan and Sophia had known about the surprise for the last two weeks, and had worked hard to keep it a secret.

Maria smiled the rest of the night. She'd never been happier. And the Indians even beat the Clippers, 3-0.

10

Good Boy

"What's the story on this one?" Michelle asked casually to Mike, who was mucking the stall of a big bay Thoroughbred early on a summer morning that promised to drift into a hot and sticky afternoon.

"Be careful; he bites and kicks," Mike warned her. "He's the only stallion on the place."

"He won't kick me," Michelle said softly, but she didn't move into the stall.

She'd offered carrot pieces and a pleasant "Hello" to each horse on site during her first day at the rundown Staten Island stable about a month ago, when she and her husband began boarding their two horses there. The big Thoroughbred had been the only horse to ignore her, turning his rump towards her and her offering. Since then she'd been wearing him down with pieces of carrot and apple. Now when she stuck treats between the boards of his stall he took them carefully, like a stray dog unsure if it should trust anyone.

"Yeah, right," Mike said, unconvinced. "He has family ties, if you know what I mean, but his owner hasn't been around lately."

About a week earlier Michelle had become enlightened to some of the clientele who boarded horses here. She hadn't known it was a mafia hangout when she signed the papers for what she hoped would only be a temporary stay for her Appendix Quarter Horse, Stallone, and her husband's Tennessee Walker, Johnny. The owner of her former barn in New Jersey had died unexpectedly, and all the boarders had to find other accommodations for their horses. Michelle was still looking for a better barn in New Jersey, but this place was convenient to the condo she and her husband rented on Staten Island, and they could afford the board. She thought as long as she oversaw things daily, it would do until she could find something better. It was a lot to take on though, since she worked part-time and also volunteered at a handicapped-riding center in New Jersey.

More than a week ago she discovered members of the mob frequented her new barn. She'd noticed there was always a telephone repair truck at the end of the street, so she innocently asked Mike's wife, Candy, if she was having telephone problems.

"That's not the telephone company; that's the FBI, keeping track of the mob," Candy had informed her. "The barn is bugged, but don't worry; they know you're not connected."

Michelle had been extra careful from that point on, but so far she'd seen no signs of any trouble except for the status of the big bay Thoroughbred, who was bored.

"How long has this horse been standing in this stall without going out?" she pressed Mike.

"I don't know for sure, but it's been awhile," Mike admitted. "The last time they turned him out in the ring he ran around a lot, bucked, and tore down the fence."

Michelle wanted to ask him exactly when that had occurred, but she knew she had to go slowly. Keeping an otherwise healthy horse locked in a stall for months at a time was cruelty to animals, but if she accused Mike of that she wasn't going to have him as an ally, and she needed him to agree to let her help.

"If I hand-walked him around the ring every day so he got a chance to stretch his legs, do you think that would help? I'd be glad to do that."

Mike remained silent and dumped the smelly contents of his blue plastic muck bucket into the wheelbarrow at the stall's door, in front of Michelle. She noticed a horse racing newspaper was stuck in the left-rear pocket of his jeans, and a couple of horses were circled in a lineup.

"Like I said, he's connected, but I don't know about anything I don't see," he said.

"Thank you," Michelle said. "By the way, what's his name?"

"Major."

The following morning, while Mike was busy working in another area of the barn, Michelle took one of Stallone's nylon halters and a lead line, along with a supply of carrots, and threw open the latch on the sliding door to Major's stall.

"Hi there, boy!" she said. "It's a beautiful morning for a walk!"

Major looked at her, craned his neck, bared his teeth like he was preparing to bite, and rolled his eyes so she could see their whites. He turned on his powerful haunches, as if he was getting ready to kick.

Michelle ignored his threats and offered him some carrots. He didn't take them, but he lowered his neck and looked a little more at ease, as if he might relent.

Michelle wondered if she should try grooming him first or walking him first. She decided on the latter, since she didn't know how he'd behave on crossties, and walking him was her priority.

Major didn't lower his head for her to put the halter on him, but he didn't move away from her, either.

"Good boy," Michelle murmured to him constantly. She patted his neck, savoring the rich smell of horse.

She stood by his left side, clicked her lead line onto the side buckle of the halter, took a tight hold of the lead line, and hoped for the best.

She got it. Major stopped at the threshold of his stall as if he was questioning if this was happening, but he let Michelle go first and followed her dutifully down the aisle of the barn and out the path to the outdoor riding arena.

'Arena' was a stretch because it was only a dirt oval rimmed by a wire fence, but it was all that was available so Michelle went for it. If Major got away from her, at least he'd be in the ring instead of flying down the street.

She was worried the most about opening the big metal gate to the ring without scaring him. He balked while she opened it and whinnied, but stood still until she led him into the ring, turned, and fastened the gate once again.

And then they walked. It was early enough no one else was using the ring, and Michelle took advantage of every second she had. She walked Major around the ring clockwise 10 times, and then she circled him and walked him around the ring counter-clockwise 10 times. At first he pranced beside her with his head high in his excitement, blowing air in and out of his nostrils like a racehorse that had given it his all. He twitched his tail too, conveying his excitement and suggesting he might bolt. But he didn't pull the lead line out of Michelle's grasp, and by their twentieth lap he was walking beside her like a proper lead-line pony in a halter class.

"That's a good start," Mike told her after he approached the fence.

Michelle hadn't seen him arrive, but she was glad he was there because she wanted the session to end well, and she was still a little worried about the metal gate.

"Would you open the gate for us, please?"

"Sure," he said, and moved to do so.

Major and Michelle passed through it, and retraced their path back to the barn and his stall. She pulled the stall door closed before she took the halter and lead line off him, reassuring him with her voice. She fed him three big carrots, turned her back, and slipped out of his stall.

The following day she repeated the process, with similar results. On the third day she had more time, so she added a thorough grooming session to the order of business. She was appalled at the amount of thrush in his left front foot, although all four needed attention. She applied thrush medicine and was grateful Major didn't seem to mind anyone picking up his feet. Somewhere along the line, he had received some good training.

The following day Michelle asked Mike if Major was current with his shots and wormers, and was pleased to hear he was. She also asked Mike if he knew about how old he was.

"I'm not sure; maybe around 4 or 5," Mike said. "His owner doesn't mind paying the bills; he just doesn't come around much."

"Who owns him, anyway?"

"Vito Russo, Emilio Russo's son."

Even naïve Michelle had heard of Emilio Russo. The mafia boss operated out of one of the Italian restaurants by the docks in Brooklyn, and his name was often in the newspapers.

Michelle kept up her horse-walking duties for a solid two weeks before she trusted Major enough to let him loose in the ring on his own. Their only audience was Pal, a stray border collie who hung out at the barn and carried rocks in his mouth like they were balls.

The walking had done the trick. This time when Major realized he was free to roam in the ring, instead of galloping around madly he trotted to the center of the ring, sank into the soft sand, and rolled repeatedly. He stood, shook the sand off his back, and circled the ring at a collected canter three times before coming to a halt in front of Michelle, a contented look in his big brown eyes.

"Good boy," she told him as she patted his neck. "That felt great, didn't it?"

Later that afternoon a part-time worker at the stable who had started recently, Conor, approached Michelle. He had a brogue, and when Michelle pressed, he said he was from Dublin. He was slim and quiet, and Michelle had seen he was a hard worker. He had curly, light-brown hair and heavy black glasses that made him look a little geeky, but he seemed to love horses. He told Michelle he used to ride regularly, and he asked her if she knew of any owners at the stable who might agree to have him exercise their horses for free.

"I might," Michelle told him, "but Mike would have to OK it."

That's how Mike came to call Vito one night to inquire if he'd mind if Conor gave Major some exercise on the trails around the stable.

"Horses aren't like boats, Vito," Mike explained. "They need exercise and daily attention."

"The last time he was turned out in the ring, he busted through the fence," Vito reminded him. "That cost me $500."

"A girl at the stable made friends with him, and he isn't doing that anymore."

Vito stalled, but he finally gave his permission, provided Conor used his own tack.

"Thanks, Vito," Mike told him. "You're helping both Major and Conor."

Conor had some tack of his own, and Michelle provided what he was missing. The first time they tacked Major up, Michelle learned Conor had worked as an exercise rider for a stable in Ireland, and he had a good seat.

Major flourished with the attention and the almost daily work. When he jumped a wide downed tree with plenty of room to spare, jumping became part of his routine. Michelle worked with the pair in the ring too, setting up small jumps the stable had on hand.

"You know, Conor, there is a little horse show over the bridge in New Jersey next weekend, and they have a hunter-jumper class," Michelle told him one afternoon as summer was drawing to an end. "We'll have to get permission from Vito, but Linda Palmer is going to it, and she'll have an open spot in her trailer."

Linda Palmer had a Quarter Horse she rode in area horse shows.

Conor looked at her before responding. "Do you think Vito will let us go?" he asked. "Be honest."

"All we can do is ask."

Mike was asked to make another call to Vito for permission, which was granted. By that time Vito had lost most of his interest in horses, but he was still paying his board bill without fail.

Early the next Saturday morning, Michelle and Conor groomed Major to perfection. Major balked when they asked him to go into the trailer, but with plenty of encouragement from Michelle and Conor, he hesitantly went inside for the short trip.

Once at the other stable, Conor tacked him up and rode him away from the other horses, onto the trails, for an easy jog. It worked wonders, as Major was as relaxed as possible for his first horse show. He won a blue ribbon, to the surprise of nearly everyone.

When they arrived back at the barn on Staten Island and put Major back in his stall, a stranger with a bandaged left hand stepped out of the shadows towards them.

"He did well, didn't he?" said the young man with a heavy New York accent. "I'm Vito Russo," he added quietly.

Michelle and Conor looked at each other, trying their best to remain calm.

"He's coming along," Michelle said. "Conor is a good rider."

"He looks good," Vito answered, still speaking of the horse.

"I think he's happy," Michelle agreed.

"You can ride him as much as you want, and take him to as many shows as you want," Vito said. "I'm too busy to fool with him right now."

"Great!" Conor said, and it was set.

"What did you do to your hand?" Michelle had to ask.

"Ah, nothing; just a little accident," Vito said, and he was gone.

Conor kept working with Major, and at the very end of summer they entered him in an A-rated horse show in the area. Vito showed up with a tacky blonde on his arm, and seemed to enjoy playing the role of show-horse owner. Michelle and Conor wondered how he even knew about it, since neither of them had spoken to him. They entered Major in two classes, and he took blue ribbons in both.

That same evening, after Major was safe in his stall and enjoying some carrots out of a small bucket Michelle was holding, Mike stuck his head in the stall.

"I thought that horse would kick you to hell and back that first day," he admitted.

Michelle just smiled. She found it hard to believe the cruelty bestowed on some animals by unknowing or uncaring people. She was glad she had stepped in so Major didn't have to endure a life in solitary confinement through no fault of his own.

11

What If?

Nine-year-old Matt Thompson drew a wavy line in the sand with the toe of his right flip-flop as he sat on a concrete bench on the beach near his seaside home in Florida. Although it was well over an hour since dinner, the July sun was still baking everything in sight. Matt had already completed his mandatory 45 minutes of practice on his trumpet, but it was too hot to play in his tree house. It was even too hot to swim in the family's pool. He didn't feel like playing any of his video games, either.

Summer camp was still a month away. He didn't know if his dad would be home from his job overseas to take them on a summer vacation this year or not. His best friend, Billy, was in Arizona visiting his grandmother. There was no one to play with other than his little sister, Jessica, who was annoying because she followed him around all the time. He could see her spying on him from some tall grass in the sand, a little behind the bench where he was sitting. She was squatting in the grass, like a Florida panther poised to pounce.

Matt's shoulders drooped as he continued to make patterns in the sand with the toe of his flip-flop. The only reason he even noticed the old black man walking toward him was that a seagull swooped a little too close once, breaking his fixation with the sand and making him look towards the surf. The smell of seaweed and wet sand filled the air, but it was so par for the course to Matt he didn't even notice it. He didn't notice the whale coming up for air periodically on the horizon either, or the small alligator keeping cool in a drainage ditch a few yards away.

"May I join you?" the man asked. He took Matt's half-smile as an affirmative, and sat on the bench to Matt's right.

"What did you do today?" the man asked him, pleasantly. He was wearing tan shorts, a yellow and orange shirt with tropical plants on it, sandals, aviator sunglasses, and a wide-brimmed straw hat. He carried a bamboo cane, which didn't help much in the sand. He had lots of little skin tags on his face and neck, and his head was covered in tight, steely gray curls.

"Nothing," Matt said dully. "There's nothing to do around here."

"Nothing to do?" the man responded, incredulous. "I find that hard to believe. This is Florida! The Sunshine State!"

"I guess."

"Ah; you're bored," said the man, stating the obvious. Just then his cane slipped from his side and fell onto the sand. Matt quickly picked it up and handed it back to him.

"Thank you," he said. "I get bored sometimes too, but when I do, I play the 'What If?' game."

"What's that?"

"Well, life is full of possibilities, and the 'What If?' game helps me to use my imagination to see them," the man said. "By the way, I should introduce myself; my name is Jonas Jefferson, like the third president of these great United States, who may or may not have been a relation."

The man twisted his body and stuck out his large right hand. Matt shook it shyly.

"My name is Matt Thompson."

"It's nice to meet you, Master Matthew Thompson," Mr. Jefferson replied formally. "I assume you live in that beautiful house behind us, and the little girl hiding in the grass behind us is your sister?"

"Yes to both," Matt admitted. "Her name is Jessica."

"Good," Mr. Jefferson said. Matt wondered what was so good about it.

"Now, where was I?" Mr. Jefferson asked. "Oh yes, the 'What If?' game. When I'm bored, I try to think about different alternatives to things. It sparks my imagination. It makes me use my brain a little, which is always good. Sometimes it makes me wonder about something enough to do a little research, and I learn something new."

"How do you play?"

"Well, there are no rules, and there is no senseless killing like in the video games you like to play," Mr. Jefferson said.

"How do you know I like to play video games?"

"That's another game I like called the 'Power of Observation,'" Mr. Jefferson answered. "You're wearing a T-shirt with a video-game character on it, and I can see you have quick reflexes by the way you picked up my cane. But I digress; I was explaining the 'What If?'" game."

He reached into the right-side pocket of his shorts and pulled out a flat, silver disc. It looked like a coin or a button, but it had no shank or holes. A faint, six-point star was etched on its head.

"Do you see this button?" he asked Matt, who nodded affirmatively.

"What if this button was not your normal button, but what if I had picked it up in the sand a little bit ago after it had been under the beach for many, many years?" he asked. "What if this button had been on the shirt of an ex-slave who fought in the Civil War? What if this silver button saved the soldier's life when it took a bullet from a sharpshooter waiting in an outcropping of rocks? What, even with a bad leg injury that would force him to use a cane the rest of his life, the soldier went on to become an informant to the Union army, and helped bring an end to slavery in our country once and for all?"

"Wow!" Matt picked the flat disc out of Mr. Jefferson's hand and fingered it.

"Now you try," Mr. Jefferson said.

"What if you bought this button yesterday on the clearance rack at Walmart?" Matt responded.

"I think you can do better than that," Mr. Jefferson said, disapprovingly.

"OK; I'll try again," Matt grinned. He paused a minute to think, and said, "What if this button isn't a button at all, but it's what is left of a screw that fell off a rocket that took off for Mars from Cape Canaveral last month?" he asked. "The star is for the United States, like on our flag."

"There you go! That's better!" Mr. Jefferson said.

At that point, Jessica bounced up.

"What if the button is made of pure silver, and it was in a treasure chest a pirate buried on the beach?" she asked breathlessly.

"That's good!" Mr. Jefferson said with a twinkle in his eye.

The trio was silent as each person considered his own thoughts.

"Were there a lot of slaves in Florida during the Civil War?" Matt asked.

"Yes, nearly half of the people who lived in Florida at that time were slaves," Mr. Jefferson said.

"We talked about the Civil War a little in social-studies class," Matt continued. "We'll study it more when we go back to school in the fall. We learned a little about the battle of Gettysburg, though."

"Yes, that was the turning point of the war, and a costly battle," Mr. Jefferson said.

"Were there any Civil War battles around here?" Matt asked.

"There weren't many Civil War battles in Florida at all," Mr. Jefferson replied. "It wasn't well populated, and its major role was to provide food for the Confederacy. But there were a few battles, like the Battle of Olustee, near Lake City, and a lot of skirmishes," he added.

"How do you know so much about the Civil War?" Matt wanted to know.

"I find it interesting," he answered. "The Union had a blockade around the entire state of Florida, trying to keep the food and supplies out of the hands of the Southern army. There were a lot of deserters in Florida during the Civil War too."

"What's a deserter?" Matt scratched a mosquito bite on his leg.

"That's a coward who quits the army without permission," Mr. Jefferson said. "There were lots of deserters from both sides who stayed in Florida until the war was over. Most of them weren't good people."

Matt and Jessica's mother called them to come in.

"You better go," Mr. Jefferson said. "It was nice talking to you. I'll sit awhile and enjoy the surf, and then I'll have to go too."

"Good-bye, Mr. Jefferson," Matt said politely. "It was nice talking with you."

"Yes, good-bye," Jessica echoed.

Mr. Jefferson smiled and nodded, and Matt and Jessica headed for their house.

They never saw Mr. Jefferson on the beach again, and they wondered where he went.

"What if he died?" Matt said.

"I don't like that 'what if,'" Jessica said flatly. "Try again."

"What if he was visiting his brother in Florida for a few days, and now he's back in Washington, D.C., where he works at the Smithsonian taking care of Civil War stuff?" Matt suggested.

"That's better," Jessica replied, and they grinned.

12

Lead Us Not Into Temptation

The man squeezing the mangoes at the Brevard County Farmers' Market in Melbourne, Florida, that hot Thursday afternoon in July was easily the most handsome man Liz Thompson had ever seen. With his tan Dockers and beige blazer over a pastel-green sports shirt, he was overdressed for a farmers' market. As she wondered if he was an actor or a model, he noticed her looking at him, and flashed her a killer smile. Then he walked six short steps towards her, pulled her toward him in a passionate embrace, and kissed her hard on the mouth.

Liz struggled to regain her senses. She had stopped off at the farmers' market to pick up some green peppers, which she planned to stuff with meatloaf for dinner after picking up her two children following an afternoon matinee at the movies.

The kiss had been shocking and yet familiar. Suddenly she realized the man was Chris Worthington. She had dated him when they were in college, but they'd broken up when she learned he was dating another girl at the same time. She hadn't seen or heard from him in 13 years.

"Chris!" she said, still groping for composure. "What are you doing in Melbourne?"

"I just transferred to Florida," he said. "I was hoping to bump into you. It's been a long time, but you look the same. You're still stunning."

"I didn't recognize you," Liz admitted, ignoring his compliment. "You had such long blond hair and a beard in college."

"Ah, we were just kids," he said, as if that explained everything. Besides regular haircuts, shaves, and manicures, he must have lost 70 pounds, gotten contacts, and had some dental work done to account for his current movie star looks.

"Are you still married to Brent Thompson?" he asked her point-blank.

"Yes, happily married and with two kids: a boy, Matt, who is 9, and a little girl, Jessica, who just turned 7," Liz reported. "How about you?"

"I never married," he said, looking deep into her eyes. "I never could find anyone who could hold a candle to the girl that got away."

Liz smiled shyly, looked at the floor, and switched subjects. "How are your parents?"

"They're fine," he said, pleased to have been asked. "Dad finally retired, and they moved south of Orlando, which is why I asked for a transfer to our Florida office on Merritt Island."

"You had been in California?"

"California first, and then Colorado." Chris put his sunglasses on top of his head. "I would love to get caught up; are you free for dinner?"

"Not tonight, I'm afraid, but I could meet you on Saturday night."

"Where's Brent?" Chris asked quickly.

"He's in China," Liz explained. "He's an architect for a company that does a lot of work overseas, so he's gone a lot."

"That must be hard," Chris said sympathetically.

"It's not easy, but we make it work."

"Well, shall we say dinner at 8 on Saturday at the place of your choosing? I'll pick you up at 7:30, if you'll make the reservation and show me how to get there."

"I should give you my address too," Liz said.

"I have that," Chris said softly. "I'll see you on Saturday at 7:30!"

"OK," Liz said, wondering why she had said yes so quickly.

Chris gave her a peck on the cheek, squeezed her hand, said "Until Saturday, then," and was gone as fast as a celebrity avoiding the paparazzi.

It didn't take Liz long to regret making the dinner date. She had second thoughts in the car while she was going to pick up her kids. But she didn't have any of Chris's contact information, so she couldn't cancel.

When she told her neighbor, Marjorie, she was going to have dinner with an old friend from college who was in town, Marjorie responded like she'd hope she would. She invited Matt and Jessica to her home for dinner and a sleepover on Saturday night with her own two children, who were about the same age.

Liz let her surprised assistant handle two real-estate showings by herself that Saturday. Liz already had an appointment with her hair-dresser early that Saturday afternoon, and she called and added a man-icure to be scheduled right after the haircut. She debated about what to wear from Thursday night until it was time to get showered and changed on Saturday night, finally choosing a simple black dress, black sandals with a mid-length cork heel and thin leather straps, and a set of sterling silver and malachite jewelry that matched the green flecks in her brown eyes. She added a small malachite hair comb to her simple brunette bob.

I'm being silly, she thought as she took one last look in the full-length mirror attached to the back of her bedroom closet.

Chris pulled up on time in a rented white Porsche convertible, and he produced a bouquet of daisies for her when she answered the doorbell.

"You shouldn't have," she told him as they walked to the kitchen together so she could get a vase for the flowers. *This feels like a date instead of a reunion,* she thought.

"I remembered you love daisies," he replied.

He held open doors for her every chance he had. Liz felt a little strange about that at first, but decided he was just being a gentleman, and tried to relax and enjoy it.

She had made reservations for them at the best seafood restaurant in town, and they ordered appetizers, wine, their entrees, and dessert.

While they ate, they got caught up. Liz learned Chris worked for a leading 3D printing company that had a big contract with NASA. The company's office on Merritt Island was used to service that contract, plus continual research and development. It was obvious Chris was doing well, but he'd never been hurting for money. His father was a former U.S. Senator, and owned a busy accounting firm.

"Additive manufacturing is the wave of the future, Liz," Chris told her.

He already knew Liz was a real estate agent, and he teased her a little about her marketing campaign.

"I couldn't miss your billboard on the road into town," he said, blue eyes twinkling. "Who wouldn't buy a house from you with that smile?"

Liz smiled, but ignored the compliment.

They enjoyed getting caught up, and reminiscing about college. Liz hadn't thought about some of their escapades in school for years.

When they left the restaurant, neither of them wanted the evening to end. Since Chris didn't know the area well, Liz directed him to drive to a small park overlooking the Atlantic. Although it was dark, they could see and hear the white foam of the waves as they curled and broke onto the beach, rolling as steadily as time passes.

Chris put the Porsche into park and turned off the engine, but let the stereo system continue to play an oldies station that was featuring Sinatra. It was windy, and the powerful breakers' driving, rhythmic beat was like a passionate Latin tango.

Liz suddenly regretted her suggestion to come here. It was innocent, but now it seemed far too sensual. She turned to the right to look out of the passenger-side window. A dark hill of sand topped with sea grasses loomed to the right of the parking lot.

Chris took Liz's left hand in his right hand, made a circle with his thumb over her knuckles, and asked her to listen to him carefully.

"Liz, I don't want to cause any trouble for you, but I do want you to know I never got over you," he told her. "If there is ever any chance for us to be together, please let me know."

"Oh, Chris," Liz began. "I know what I should say, and what I will say. I'm not the girl you knew in college anymore. I'm a married woman. I'm committed to my husband and my family. We have our problems like everyone else, but I won't do anything to jeopardize my family. But there should be a picture of you, my friend, in the Bible under the passage, 'And lead us not into temptation.'"

Chris smiled sadly, brought her hand to his mouth, and kissed it softly.

"Brent is a lucky man," he told her. "And now, I better get you home."

When they arrived at the large, oceanfront home, Chris walked her to the front door, but only gave her a peck on the cheek to say good-bye. "I know there are probably neighbors watching, and I have to let you go," he said as she punched in the security code on the door's electronic lock, nodded, let herself into the house, and watched him return to his car and drive away.

Liz took her shoes off at the door, and walked to the kitchen. The daisies were on the counter where she'd left them. She buried her nose in the blossoms, took a deep breath, and then headed upstairs, lost in thought. Thankfully the wine she'd had at dinner helped her to sleep.

Liz thought about the evening often during the next two weeks, and had to will herself to concentrate on her regular duties and chores when her thoughts drifted. At dinner Chris had given her his business card containing his e-mail address and cell phone number, but he didn't contact her again and she didn't contact him, either.

Liz knew she'd done the right thing, but she hadn't had that kind of attention from any man in some time.

Not even from Chris, when I knew him in college, she admitted. *And rarely from Brent, either. I guess we're in a little slump. But dependability is more important than flattery.*

It's hard to run the household and raise two kids with a primarily absentee father, even though Brent does the best he can when he is home.

Sometimes we need him to be here though, Liz thought. *Like I need him, right now.*

That's why the woman who was so good at arranging schedules

for everyone else finally took more than a few hours for herself. Brent had plenty of frequent-flyer miles, so she decided to use some of them to fly to China to be with him for five days.

She chose a week in early August for her trip, as Matt would be away in summer camp. She asked her in-laws to take care of Jessica that same week. She had her assistant take over for her at work, and she arranged for Marjorie to take care of the family cat.

Brent and Liz hadn't had so much time together alone since their honeymoon. Brent had to work each day, but Liz spent that time reading and napping in his hotel room. They went out to dinner at the best restaurants in the city each night. On the night before she flew home, they dressed up and went to their hotel's Chinese version of a jazz club.

"This is hilarious," Liz giggled as they listened to a three-piece band of Oriental musicians try to perform the music of Duke Ellington. The leader's introductions to each piece, spoken in Chinese, were in stark contrast to the musical repertoire.

"I don't care; may I have this dance?" Brent replied, reaching for her hand.

As they swayed to a peculiar sound coming from a saxophone, Liz sighed in contentment, knowing she was where she was supposed to be. Brent wasn't as handsome or demonstrative as Chris, but he worked hard, he was dependable, and he was devoted to her and the family their love had built. Their marriage had challenges, but they were a team.

Brent dipped his head and gave his wife a tender kiss as they danced. "I'm so glad I married you," she whispered.

13

Make It Happen

"Any progress yet on connecting with the director of marketing for Wolf Oil?" Al Saunders asked after poking his head into Bobby Gaines' tiny office at Saunders' Chevy dealership in the heart of Central Pennsylvania. An old-fashioned electric fan whirled away on Bobby's black metal desk, since it was a hot July afternoon and the building's air conditioning didn't work well in its interior offices.

"Not yet; I've been trying every day for weeks, but I haven't been able to get past his secretary."

"Keep trying; I've been talking to one of their vice presidents for a couple years, and he said they have money to spend and the timing might finally be right," Al said. "Also, Gary Griffith said to tell them if they'll sponsor us, he'll switch to Wolf Oil for his fleet of trucks to sweeten the deal. And I want you to catch up to Kevin Whitaker as soon as you can too. See what you think of him both as a driver and as a person, and let me know if you think he would be a good fit with our program."

"Yes, sir."

Finding sponsorship money for a World of Outlaws (WoO) sprint car team was a tall order, but Bobby was doing the best he could to follow every lead. He'd been a sprint car driver himself until a career-ending accident had left him with many injuries and an addiction to his pain medication. He'd been through rehab, and now his team at a local pain-management clinic controlled every pill that went into his mouth. A recent nerve block had helped a little, and he was seeing some benefits in acupuncture and aquatic therapy. Landing the job as the team manager of Al Saunders' new WoO team was a godsend to his confidence and a major step back towards normalcy. He didn't want to do anything to jeopardize the opportunity.

He was done leaving messages with the secretary of Wolf Oil's director of marketing though. Tom Coy's direct work number didn't seem to be published anywhere. Bobby had left plenty of messages with Coy's assistant. It appeared the man was never going to return his calls, so he would have to find a way around it.

The number for the main switchboard at Wolf Oil's headquarters in Manhattan was (212) 555-9000. Bobby's sprint car number used to be 19. He picked up his cell phone, dialed (212) 555-9019, and wondered whom he'd get. With any luck, it wouldn't be someone's voice mail.

"Hoover," a masculine voice answered.

Bobby pretended to be agitated. "Damn!" he said. "I was just talking to Tom Coy in marketing, and I got disconnected and connected to you by mistake. You know how the phones are around here. Would you mind reconnecting me to him?"

"Sure," Hoover said, aiming to please. "Just give me a minute." A few seconds passed. "His extension is 9224; let me transfer you."

"Thanks a lot," Bobby said and scribbled the number on his notepad for future use.

Five seconds later, Tom Coy picked up the phone on his desk on the first ring.

"Good morning, Mr. Coy," Bobby began. "Your boss and my boss, Al Saunders, are business acquaintances, and they would like me to outline a program we're sure would be an excellent avenue to use to promote Wolf Oil next year. I'll be in Manhattan all next week. Could I have an hour of your time on say next Tuesday, July 19th, in your office at 11 a.m.?"

Bobby didn't have any plans to be in New York. He was fudging as smoothly as one of Al Saunders' used-car salesmen.

Tom Coy looked through his office door to see where his secretary was, but she was away from her desk. He needed to be in the main conference room in less than 5 minutes for a meeting. He had no idea who this guy was, but he could get rid of him easily enough next Tuesday if necessary, so he took the meeting.

"Well, OK," he said, hesitantly. "What did you say your name was?"

"Bobby Gaines, with the Al Saunders family of car dealerships in Pennsylvania."

"I saw you called a few times," Tom admitted. "OK; we'll get to the bottom of this next Tuesday, but it'll have to be at 2 p.m."

"Thank you, sir; I'll see you then," Bobby replied, and hung up before he could change his mind.

Bobby hated cities. He also wasn't fond of public transportation of any type, so he drove from Pennsylvania to Manhattan the day before the planned meeting and stayed in a hotel two blocks from the office building that night. His blond hair was freshly cut. The next morning he put on his brand-new suit and dress shoes. The latter had heels of differing heights to compensate for the fact one leg was shorter than the other one following the operations he had after his crash.

He had a small rolling briefcase containing his laptop computer. He knew his PowerPoint presentation forwards and backwards, but he was still as nervous as a rookie in his first race at 1:45 p.m. when he approached the receptionist's desk on the 40th floor of the office building containing Wolf Oil's corporate headquarters.

"I'm Bobby Gaines," he told the receptionist. "I have a 2 o'clock with Tom Coy."

The receptionist held up a finger as she made a call, spoke a few words to the person on the other end, and told Bobby "Mr. Coy's assistant will come to get you, Mr. Gaines."

Bobby had visions of a burly man coming, grabbing him by the arm, and shoving him back onto the elevator, out the door, and to the curb. Instead, a petite Oriental woman whose voice he immediately recognized as Coy's secretary appeared.

She peered at him through enormous black-framed eyeglasses and studied him like a seal waiting for a cue to do a trick in exchange for a fish. "Mr. Gaines, please follow me; I'll take you to Mr. Coy," she said briskly.

Tom Coy turned out to be nice, and a race fan to boot. He was short, with trim brown hair and gold, wire-framed glasses. He looked more like a golfer than a race fan, but there were large, framed photos of an Indy car, a sports car, and a dragster on the walls of his office. Bobby used them as conversation starters.

"Mr. Gaines, why exactly are you here?" Tom said a few minutes later.

"I want Wolf Oil to be the primary sponsor of Al Saunders' World of Outlaws sprint car team next year."

"And why should we do that?"

"Because it would give you exposure to race fans you've never reached before, in a national series that races from coast to coast before grassroots fans that actually change their own oil and care about what kind of oil goes into their cars," Bobby told him. "We also have a business-to-business partnership to discuss with you that would see a large fleet of over-the-road trucks switch to your brand of lubricants over your competition's."

He launched into the key points of his presentation from memory.

Tom didn't say a word throughout Bobby's pitch. He remained silent for a full minute afterward.

Bobby had been close to dying more than once in his life. He figured this was yet another time as the seconds ticked by while he waited for a response.

"I'll tell you what I'm going to do," Tom said slowly. "I am the director of marketing for Wolf Oil, but I don't make decisions like this myself. I have a committee I depend on to help ensure we spend the company's marketing dollars as wisely as possible.

"I will give you a half-hour slot to make a presentation to the entire marketing committee next month. We'll hear all the presentations that week, consider all the pluses and minuses of each one, and make our decision. You can schedule your time slot with Wendy, my assistant, on your way out. Thanks for coming in."

Bobby wasn't sure what to think about the way the message had been delivered. He didn't know if it was an elaborate brush off or an actual opportunity, but he quickly decided to consider it to be the latter. He thanked Tom, shook his hand, and said he'd see him soon.

Tom walked him out of his office and together they stopped at the Oriental lady's cubicle.

"Wendy, please schedule Mr. Gaines in for a half-hour presentation during our marketing week in August," he told her, and disappeared.

Bobby left with an appointment card containing a date and a time. He drove back to Pennsylvania later that afternoon, and when he told

Al Saunders about the encounter the following morning, his boss was pleased with his results.

"Now maybe you can check out Kevin Whitaker," he told him. "He's racing at Eldora this weekend. Don't let him know we're considering offering him the ride. Just check him out and let me know what you think. And good job, Bobby."

"Yes, sir," Bobby told him. "And thank you."

Bobby's first choice for a driver would have been his friend, Trevor Anthony, but Trevor was happy with his current team, and he didn't want to travel as much as the Outlaws did.

Kevin Whitaker drove for a small, family team with limited funding, but a few people had already noticed what he'd done with substandard equipment. He wasn't running for points anywhere this year, but was picking and choosing between WoO, All Star, and Central Pennsylvania shows.

Bobby had planned to attend a classic car show near his home that weekend, but found himself in rural Ohio instead. As luck would have it, the hotel he booked was hosting several of the traveling teams that weekend, including Whitaker's. Five rigs were in the parking lot, but it was raining cats and dogs when Bobby checked in. His body always ached more when it rained. The woman who was running the reception desk noticed the checkered flag embossed on his wallet when he pulled out his credit card, and she assigned him a room in the same wing of the hotel as the other racers.

It wasn't hard to find Kevin's room. When Bobby walked past it on his way to his own room, the door was open and Kevin himself was grooving tires in it. He'd put a sheet from the bed on the carpet to catch the debris. An electrical cord was running from the bathroom to where he was working in the hotel room's foyer. Seven tires were piled up beside the door. He was working on the eighth, which was lying on a luggage rack.

Bobby proceeded to his room, put his suitcase and computer bag in it, turned on the air conditioner, and went back into the hall. He made sure his door was locked, and walked back towards Kevin's room.

"Interesting work area," he deadpanned as he leaned a shoulder against the open door of Kevin's room.

"Yeah, for sure," Kevin said, pausing for a moment. "We'll clean it up good." He was tall, with short brown hair, blue eyes, and a quick smile. He reminded Bobby of a lanky soldier from World War II. "We were lucky enough to win a couple races lately, so we were able to buy some new tires. Usually we use the ones the big teams throw away. I didn't want to groove them outside in the rain, or wait to do it at the track if it ever stops raining."

Then Kevin realized to whom he was talking.

"Hey, you're Bobby Gaines, aren't you? Nice to meet you! You're a legend!"

"Thanks," Bobby said, and shook Kevin's outstretched hand. "Do you think we'll get rained out tonight?"

"I don't know; it's supposed to clear off, but you can never tell."

That's when Bobby noticed the Chevy engine in the hotel room's bathtub.

"You're going for hotel guest of the year, I see," he said.

"Yeah; we could have worked on the engine at somebody's shop I guess, but Joe doesn't want anyone to see it too closely; he doesn't want anyone to know his secrets," Kevin said, smiling.

"I see," Bobby said. "Do you need any help?"

"Nah, we're OK, but thanks!"

The races at Eldora Speedway were delayed for an hour that night due to the earlier rain, but the show did get in. The push truck drivers did a heroic job to get the track run in as quickly as possible. The rain did nothing to reduce the humidity hanging in the air though, and the line for drinks at the concession stands remained long all night.

Kevin started sixth in his heat, took the lead on lap five, and won going away. He had to start fifth in the dash, but he got to third before the checkered fell to earn the inside starting spot in Row 2 for the 30-lap feature.

He ran in third for the first 10 laps of the main event, but made a mistake and fell two positions. With the help of one restart, he made them up within four laps to regain third place. Second place was a gift when that driver suffered a flat right-rear tire with five laps to go. He took the lead with two to go with as nifty a pass as Bobby had ever seen. He built his lead from that point on.

In victory lane he thanked his sponsors and his crew, the track's staff, and all the fans for coming and being patient during the late start.

Bobby hung around Kevin's pit area until the bitter end. Kevin didn't stop signing autographs and letting kids sit in his car until the last fan left, which was a good hour after the show was over.

He'll do, Bobby thought as he drove back to the hotel. *Now let's see if I can find us some money.*

About the Author

Linda Mansfield is an award-winning reporter, editor, author, and public relations representative. She is a former editor at a Manhattan publishing house. She was the first female editorial staff member of "National Speed Sport News," and her work appears regularly in its successor, "Speed Sport Magazine." She owns Restart Communications, a public relations agency based in Indianapolis.

Her first collection of fictional short stories, "Stories for the 12 Days of Christmas," was published in 2015. In 2017 she is releasing three sequels: "Twelve Stories for Spring," "Twelve Stories for Summer," and "Twelve Stories for Fall." All four books stand alone; there are no cliffhangers or "to be continued" lines.

Summer has always been one of Mansfield's favorite seasons because her birthday comes in July. The accompanying photo shows her with her star-shaped cake on birthday number seven, right before she made her wish and blew out the candles.

These days one of her birthday wishes is that you'll enjoy her books. To learn of Mansfield's upcoming releases by e-mail, readers are encouraged to subscribe to her e-mail list through her Web site at LindaMansfieldBooks.com, and receive a free short story as her thank you.

Readers may also reach her on Facebook at "Linda Mansfield — Author," and at Twitter at @RestartLMAuthor. She has a YouTube channel and a blog too.

Reviews are important to authors. If you liked "Twelve Stories for Summer," Mansfield will be grateful if you'd leave a positive review on the Web site of the outlet where you purchased it.

Summer was the season for birthdays in the Mansfield house when Linda Mansfield was growing up. Today one of her wishes is that you'll enjoy her books.

Don't miss the other books in the "Two Good Feet" series!

1
Available now!

2
Available now!

3
Available now!

4
Fall of 2017